INVITATION

Christina Hoffman

Visit Christina Hoffman at www.christinahoffman.com
And at amazon.com/author/christinahoffman

Copyright © 2014 by Christina Hoffman

Printed in the United States of America
First Printing, 2014

ISBN: 978-0-9960967-0-6

Cover Design: Michele at The Book Cover Studio
Proofreading/Formatting: Renee Lewin Book Design and Publishing

Thank you to Colleen at https://www.facebook.com/thebooklender, for her support and generosity

For everyone still looking.

Dear Reader,

Welcome to the world of Smart and Sexy, where we prove that Heat can still be Sweet.

Thank you so much for purchasing this book. I know how precious time is these days, and I thank you for spending some of your moments enjoying this story.

This book is a work of fiction, and in the interests of the story, I have left safe sex practices out of the lives of these characters. In your own life, though, please remember to always protect yourself and others when enjoying intimate company.

Wishing you peace, pleasure and love,

TABLE OF CONTENTS

CHAPTER ONE

I can't even blame it on the booze. There wasn't any, or at least there wasn't any for me. I was with Chloe, my bodyguard. Okay, she was my friend, but a really overprotective friend who knew all about what I'd been through and wanted to make sure it never happened again. So, no alcohol.

But, what she and I hadn't counted on was *him* being there. There I was, minding my own business, putting in my time at the Med School Social, more than ready to head home for some studying, then Chinese food and a movie. And suddenly, *him*.

I was inhaling when I caught sight of him, but my breath just stopped. It felt like being punched in the chest. I kept telling myself, look away, look away! But it was impossible. I was paralyzed. His beautiful face and magnificent body were magnets, and my eyes were locked on them.

I hadn't felt this kind of physical attraction since, well, ever. I had never felt like that. I had stayed away from men for two years. I was pretty much terrified of them, to tell the truth. But there he was. Unavoidable and irresistible.

I saw him in profile. Oh, that hair. Thick, almost curly, falling into his eyes. The kind of hair you need to gently push off of his face right before you kiss him. Or, the kind of hair you grab really hard right before you're about to...

But, I'm getting ahead of myself. The point I'm trying to make is that my mind very clearly saw all the dangers ahead and was saying, "Turn around, go, get out of here! Before it's too late." But then he turned around to look right at me, and it was already too late.

We held each other's gaze a second longer than politeness required. Something inside me went click, and for the first time in almost two years, I felt young and alive, and really, really turned on. Every part of me suddenly woke up, and all the best parts started to tingle. I was breathing harder. My lips were parted slightly, already begging to be kissed.

It was overwhelming. I was out of practice. No, actually, I had never had the kind of practice you would need to stay controlled in a situation like that. I think maybe you can have a soul mate for your mind, and also one for your body. And my body was saying "Get me over there right now!"

But I was still too afraid. I smiled a little and turned away.

I had to stay at the party for at least a little while, to look sociable. I wandered over to the food table and stared at the snacks. It was already picked over; medical students love free food. All that was left were the usual crackers-and-cheese combos, and they were already stale. Nothing looked very good, and I found that my throat was too tight to eat anyway.

I was formulating a plan for escaping without the other students or the teachers noticing when I felt the air move behind me. It was the softest of breezes, a caress against my bare shoulders. Then, a hand on my back: an electric shock to my body, which was wildly pleasurable. I gasped and spun around. Right into the arms of...

"I'm Liam."

Liam. Right into the arms of Liam. Oh, he was even more beautiful up close. My hand rose all on its own to push that wonderful floppy hair from his face. I stopped suddenly, embarrassed, but he caught my wrist, and held my palm gently to his face. The world fell away. All I could see was him. All I could hear was our breathing. I looked into his eyes and knew.

"Want to get out of here?" he asked, and of course, foolish, foolish woman that I am, I said, "Yes."

I had seen him a week earlier, on my first day at the hospital. I'm a medical student and had just finished the lecture part of things where we sit around learning about chemical reactions and body parts. That was over, at last, and we were moving on to seeing real live patients in the hospital.

The orientation was step one in getting us ready for our new roles. We each got a short lab coat and a tour of the locker rooms. We picked up our I.D.'s and complained about the pictures.

I'm not exactly sure why I first noticed Liam. Since the bad thing happened, I keep my head down and make eye contact with almost nobody. I wear my hair in a tight bun at the nape of my neck and my clothes are dull and loose.

On that particular day, I was trying very hard to concentrate. I was excited to be starting work in the hospital, but I was also terrified. There was so much to take in and remember. People's lives were at stake. My head was already reeling after only two hours of the orientation. The last thing on my mind was men. So, who knows why I took that second look as he walked by our group.

Well, actually I do know why. He was gorgeous. Ridiculously gorgeous. Dark wavy hair, just slightly overgrown so he looked like a happy surfer who'd tumbled out of bed. Smiling eyes. Sparkling, mischievous, movie star eyes. A little bit of stubble, likely because he had been on call all night. The rest of him looked pretty much immaculate. He wore light wool pants and a sky blue shirt, which matched his blue eyes and forced you to notice them. No tie, but the white lab coat made him look professional enough.

I was dedicated to maintaining my nun-like lifestyle, but, seriously, it was impossible not to stare at him. Even Chloe noticed him. She looked at him, then at me. She shook her head lightly and whispered, "No". I laughed a little because she sounded like a mom telling a toddler that she couldn't have any candy. Which was pretty much what was happening, so I guess Chloe nailed that.

INVITATION

She was absolutely right. I didn't want any trouble. Certainly not that awful, frightening feeling of falling in love. No time-consuming romance. I certainly didn't want another setback like I'd had before. Even a plain old tiny heartbreak could set me back, and put me way off course in my career.

No, I didn't have the time or energy for any distractions. Nothing. Just work and school.

So I tried my best to ignore the stunning resident with the black hair, and focused instead on the tall blond giving us the orientation spiel. This was much easier because I felt no attraction to him at all. He was really handsome, too, but something about him seemed mean, or maybe arrogant. It's hard to remember exactly what I thought of him that first time, because the memory is so clouded with all that came after. I'll just say he was a tall, slim blond who should have caught my eye, but didn't.

CHAPTER TWO

Liam and I made our way through the crowds of people at the party. As we walked, I sent Chloe a text, so she wouldn't worry. I wasn't about to talk to her in person; she would have spent an hour convincing me that leaving with Liam was a terrible idea.

At the front door, we bundled up in our raincoats and scarves, and headed outside. It was March in Seattle, so it was grey and wet and cold. "Coffee?" he asked.

"Sure."

"We'll go to my favorite place."

We scurried down the street. It was too cold outside for romantic dawdling. Just as I was becoming truly frozen, Liam stopped in front of a door and opened it. "After you."

We walked into the café and made our way through the clusters of people to the counter. Liam looked back at me as we stood in line. "What can I get you?"

I wasn't used to dating and was, in many ways, new to the whole scene. I was so charmed by this person, this mature real life man, offering to pay, that I forgot the names of everything I normally like to drink. I wanted to order something, anything, but I was completely flustered. I blurted out, "Water!"

He smiled. "Water. Wow, exciting!" From someone else, with a different tone of voice, it might have sounded snide, but Liam's face was kind and his smile was sincere.

I smiled shyly and shrugged. "I'm not an exciting kind of person."

He looked into my eyes again and didn't look away. "I don't think I believe that." I was having trouble breathing properly, but just as I was becoming light-headed, he turned back to the counter to order.

I left him there and wandered over to the seating area. It was a wonderfully relaxed café with big old armchairs and sofas, most of them filled with happy chattering people. I loved the whole place instantly.

The only spot available was a love seat. Just room enough for two. I sat down and sank back into the soft cushions. After a few minutes, Liam came over. He passed me the water. "Is this acceptable, miss? I believe it was a fine year." We both laughed at the cheesy line. He was so uninterested in being cool that he was by far the coolest person I had ever met

I reached for the bottle, smiling, but he snatched it back and said, "I should probably at least know your name before we get drunk together on this water."

"I'm Madison. Maddie."

He handed me the bottle and sat down beside me. "Madison," he repeated. He was staring at me, but it was a gentle, sweet stare.

I felt nervous and insecure. "What?'

"You are just so lovely." He regretted it instantly and leaned back suddenly, covering his face with his hands. "Oh god, I'm sorry. It just slipped out. Way to play it cool, right?"

"It's okay," I said, looking down at my ugly baggy clothes, thinking about my face with no make-up. "I know you're just kidding." I wanted to let him off the hook. I tried to turn it around, to compliment him instead, since he was obviously the good-looking one of this loveseat. "But, it's okay, because you look good enough for both of us." Lord, my stupid comments were even worse than his. I was out of practice. I hadn't flirted in a long time.

He put his hand on my knee and I jumped, splashing water on us both. "Oh no," he pretended to be distressed. "This red wine will never come out. I need baking soda, or club soda, or something." My whole body relaxed and I started laughing. It was that easy happy laughter that only comes when you're with someone who just seems to fit with you.

But then, as he was brushing water droplets off his pants, he said, "I should take these off. Want to come to my house?" My chest tightened and my heart started pounding. Just like that, the spell was just broken and all the magic of the evening disappeared.

I was suddenly terrified and nauseated. I could barely think straight. Something was squeezing down on my chest and I couldn't catch my breath. I stood too suddenly, banging into the table in front of us, spilling people's drinks all over. "Oh, I'm so sorry," I said over and over again as I made my way to the door. I wanted to buy everyone another drink, but I didn't have that kind of money. Even if I did have money, I had to get out of there. I had to get out of there before I had a complete panic attack.

I ran all the way home. I was wet from the rain and frozen solid by the time I finally burst through our front door. Chloe was already there, waiting at the table. She stood up quickly and swooped down on me. I'm sure she had a great lecture all planned out, but as soon as she saw me, pale and terrified, her face changed from irritated to concerned. She helped me take my coat off – my fingers were numb from the cold -- pulled me toward the sofa.

"Are you okay?" She looked terrified. "What did he do? Who is he? Did he hurt you?"

"No," I assured her. "Not at all. He was really nice. Kind of wonderful, actually." I leaned back into the sofa. "I don't know what happened. I ran away."

"You mean you told him you needed to go home."

"No, I literally ran away. It was humiliating. Just completely awful."

I told her about all about the mini-date and its abrupt end.

INVITATION

"Well, this is just proof that you're not ready. Right?" She held my hand and waited for me to agree. "You have to give it more time."

I nodded as I stood up. I made my way towards my room. "I've got to go to bed." I turned back. "You're a good friend. I'm sorry I worried you."

I made a vow to myself that I would avoid this Liam person as much as I could from then on. I told myself that I had imagined it all: the easy, playful banter, the intense sexual attraction. I thought I had convinced myself. I felt strong and full of resolve. As I was putting on my pajamas, though, the soft cotton slid across the back of my shoulders. I shivered, remembering the breeze on my shoulders at the party. My heart skipped a beat, and my body tingled. I knew I was in deep, deep trouble.

CHAPTER THREE

The next day was my first official day of work in the hospital. I knew the layout of the hospital fairly well because I'd worked there over the summer. I had been helping out with a research project at the time. I could tantalize you by saying it was about sex, which it was, but my job was to count fruit flies to determine how often they were getting it on. *Very* sexy.

Although I had been at the hospital for a couple of months, I'd mostly been in the area where the labs were. It's an enormous hospital with many different wards, so part of the stress of the first few days was going to be finding my way around.

I needed to get to Pediatrics and wasn't sure where I was going. I spotted a young boy in a wheel chair and figured he might be headed where I needed to be. So I decided to follow him.

His little arms moved quickly, spinning the tires of his wheelchair; he made revving sounds like a racecar engine. He spun around and started back, flying towards me. He tried to run me over, but I jumped out of the way just in time. As I did so, I lifted my arm high above my head and brought it down just behind him as he passed me. I said in an excited voice, "Aaaaand, he wins his first Grand Prix! The crowd goes wild!" Then we both danced around a bit, pretending to go a little wild. He giggled happily and gave me a high five.

I was about to ask him his name, but he looked past me and slumped down in his chair. "Oh, hell," he said. I turned to see what had brought on his dark mood. It was Liam, coming towards us with a grim look on his face. I thought he was about to say something nasty about our disastrous date.

He glanced briefly at me, then at the boy. "Hey, kiddo," he said to the little boy, "you've got to go back."

"I know, I know," said the child.

Liam ignored me completely. He started walking back the way he had come, and the boy rolled slowly along behind him.

I stayed rooted to the spot, trying to remember how to breathe. Despite my attempt to wall off whatever feelings might have been developing, I was still wildly attracted to Liam. It hadn't gone away.

If anything, the attraction was more intense than ever. My whole body felt warm. It took all my control not to run up to him. I just wanted to touch him. I was like a little kid with a cake -- just one lick! Please!

I felt out of control. The fact was that he felt nothing for me anymore -- and who could blame him? I was the weirdo who runs away from really sweet guys in coffee shops -- should have been a relief, but I felt a powerful sense of loss and longing.

Nothing good could come from these feelings. Every sensible molecule in my body knew it. I had to stay away from that guy.

My good intentions lasted about a week. On that particular day, I, along with five other eager students, was following along behind a stern older doctor. She was grouchy as hell to us, but the kids seemed to love her. She was my preceptor, or boss, Dr. Olsen. Each day we did rounds on all the patients, checking on their progress, or meeting the new kids who had come in overnight.

Once again, she was explaining the cases and the lab work results to us. We were all frantically scribbling everything down or typing it into our phones, pretending to know what she was talking about. Or at least I was pretending. Maybe everyone else is a frigging genius.

We were all squeezed into a little room, learning more about my favorite Indi 500 patient, Alex. Someone bumped against me, and I assumed it was a straggler squeezing in behind me.

A tingling started down my spine. Is it possible to see without your eyes? Because my body knew instantly that it was him. It was Liam. I felt the warmth of him all down my body.

He leaned forward and whispered "Hey", right below my ear. His breath stirred the tiny hairs on my neck, making me shiver. It was the sexiest thing I had ever felt.

I turned my head a little, happy. Despite my vows of celibacy and Liam-avoidance, I was relieved that he seemed to be giving me a second chance. "I'm so sorry…" I started to say.

"Excuse me," the Dr. Olsen snapped. "Are we interrupting you, Dr. Spencer, or might I continue?"

I shook my head and apologized. My cheeks burned with embarrassment. Great start to my new career. See? There are so many ways men can be trouble.

I didn't turn my head again even a fraction of an inch. When we had finished discussing Alex's case, we said good-bye to him and turned to leave. Liam was gone, and my heart sank

Half an hour later, when we were finished rounding on the patients, I noticed Liam leaning against the nurses' station. I thought he might be the Resident in charge of us and I tried to decide if that was going to be a good or a bad thing. It was bad because I would be forced see his beautiful face every day, which would be torture. And it was good because I would get to see his beautiful face every day. I'm the first to admit I made no sense at all where Liam was concerned.

"Hi," I said. After the coffee shop disaster, I was feeling anxious and more than a little shy. "Are you our Resident?"

"Nope," he laughed. "Thank god. Who would want all that paperwork?"

His smile was killing me. I thought I could die if I didn't get to see it again, and again and again.

"I'm on Cardiology right now. I just stopped by to see race car kid."

"Oh," I laughed. "Mario Andretti?"

INVITATION

"Yeah, that's him. Alex. He's been through a lot. He's my bud."

A man who is nice to kids is such a turn on. Don't ask me why. No doubt it's some biological, primitive something-or-other. Whatever the case, that was it for me. Even though the sex appeal, which radiated off him in waves, had drawn me in, it was his kindness that finally made him completely irresistible.

He leaned toward me and whispered in my ear. "Can we talk later?" I had said yes before he had even finished the question. So much for making him work for it. Someone else would have panicked at my eagerness (aka desperation), but he just laughed and gave my hand a squeeze. It felt like I had known him forever.

CHAPTER FOUR

We met after work outside the doors of Emergency and decided to just walk around for a bit. It was a beautiful evening, warmer than a normal for March, with a bit of light remaining in the sky. We made all that compulsory getting-to-know-you small talk as we strolled through a nearby park.

He seemed happy and comfortable in his own skin: confident without being arrogant at all. He was an adult in a world filled with petulant little boys. Here was an incredibly sexy man, who, as far as I could tell, wasn't playing any games. What you saw was what you got, and oh lord, did I like what I could see.

We were crossing a bridge and stopped half way across to watch the water flow by. It's so nice to stand beside someone you really like. You can't see their eyes, so you can say things you might not otherwise say. You feel their elbow touching yours, and then you say something funny and they bang their hip into you while they laugh. Somehow, these little moments tell you most of what you need to know.

"Well, you're not only gorgeous, you're interesting."

I was suddenly at a loss for words, so I looked down at the water, smiling.

Then he asked, "Can you tell me what happened at the coffee shop?", and in that moment I felt that, yes, I could tell him. That maybe this was one person who would be all right with it all.

We pushed back from the bridge railing, and as we continued our walk, I told him about the terrible night.

18

INVITATION

Two years before, Chloe and I had gone out to meet up with my ex-boyfriend and she left with some new guy. Alone, I had consumed a roofied drink and somehow ended up online naked and humiliated. "Bad pictures, you know?"

That's all I could say, but it was enough. He got it. He shook his head and took my hand. "Come home with me," he said.

I laughed nervously. "I don't think I'm brave enough to go home with you." I used my hands to put brackets around "home with you", and wiggled my eyebrows.

Liam smiled. "That's not the only thing we can do at home."

"Well, what else?"

"Video games?"

I burst out laughing. "Good god, that sounds awful." It did, but being with Liam felt really good. I didn't want the evening to end. "But, okay."

We walked back toward the hospital and he stopped at a parked car. It was a pretty black car, an Audi I think, but I'm no expert. I had spent more than a few years on the bus, and any car was a thrill.

"Is it far?" I asked. "I thought all you residents lived close to the hospital."

"I have a dive close by that I share with a couple of guys. It's easier to be close when I'm doing a lot of Call. But I want to take you somewhere nicer."

I laughed, "Are you taking me to your parents'?" I was joking but the serious look on his face made me stop smiling. "I'm sorry. That came out wrong. I didn't mean to sound so snide. Parent issues. I'm sure yours are great."

He came over to my side of the car. I leaned back against the car while he moved closer to me. "I do live with my parents. In a way. It's nice, you'll see." Then he cupped my face and leaned forward to kiss me.

I think it was meant to be a quick, icebreaker kind of kiss, but the second our lips, I was shocked by the intensity of it.

Pleasure and desire flooded through me. My mind went blank. I wrapped my hands around his back to pull myself even closer to him. His hands started running up and down my back with increasing urgency. He pushed them up into my hair and kissed me harder.

His hands moved back down again until he was cupping my ass, and grabbing it just hard enough to increase the excitement. I thought I had buried all these feelings, but here they were, stronger than ever, absolutely bursting from me.

I kissed him everywhere I had access to. I smelled his neck and his hair, and we kissed some more. Our tongues moved in and out of our mouths, taunting each other playfully. I was wild with desire.

Finally we pulled apart and stood staring at each other. I was shocked, and he seemed to be, too. We were practically panting. "Oh my god," I murmured.

He nodded and seemed to be trying to catch his breath. "So," he said, stroking my hair. "Home?"

My head was nodding vigorously before I could even speak. My mind was still anxious and probably not quite ready for what this man had to offer, but, sweet god, my body was. "Yes. Now," was my answer.

In the car, driving along the darks street of Seattle, we tried to fill the time with small talk. It got serious pretty quickly, though. There was no way to avoid the topic. "So, the pictures and everything," he started. "You're obviously not okay with that yet."

"No. I guess that's true."

"So you haven't, you know, *been* with anyone since then?"

"I haven't even been on a date."

Here is where things got really interesting. I expected Liam to either be scared off by the pressure, or to start playing the sensitive new-age guy routine: how we didn't have to do anything, how we'd take it slow, how we'd just be friends. Instead he said, "Well, it's time you got back in the game, don't you think? Let's just have some fun. You remember fun, right?"

INVITATION

I turned my head towards him. "Well, that was unexpected!"

"But you're smiling." It was true. I should have been repulsed, or at least a bit anxious, but instead I felt something wonderful opening up inside of me. He went on, "You're gorgeous. You're incredibly sexy. Your body just fits with mine. If that kiss is anything to go by... Jesus, I shouldn't be thinking about this while I'm trying to drive." Here he took my hand. "I'm sure you have trust issues. Who doesn't, right? I'm definitely not long-term material, and I'm sure you don't want to fall in love and be vulnerable and all that, right?" I nodded, still a little confused. Was this beautiful man taking advantage of me, or understanding me completely? Was it worth the risk?

"So, let's just have some fun." He looked at me, waiting for my approval.

"Okay. We can try."

He turned back to the road, pleased with the decision. "Good, because I want to kiss every part of you."

CHAPTER FIVE

Not long after that we reached a house. It was a mansion, really, and it made me instantly uncomfortable. There was no way I was going to waltz in, say hello to Mr. and Mrs. Country Club and then head upstairs for some making out.

Liam sensed my reluctance and nodded towards the enormous four-car garage. "I live above it. I wanted to be able to stay here to save a little money, and also to get away from the mold in my apartment now and then." We walked to the far side of the garage, where stairs led up to a second level. "But I couldn't live with my parents, you know?" He pulled me gently up the stairs and started unlocking the door to his secret lair. "So I built this place for myself."

I was expecting, well, I was expecting some dusty old attic-like space with a mildewed mattress on the floor and a sagging patch in the middle of the room that we had to avoid, or risk falling through.

I was so wrong. It was a beautiful, long room with shiny hardwood floors, pale blue-grey walls, and white shutters on the windows. It was GQ man meets beach house. "Oh, it's amazing," I gushed. I spun my arms around. "How?!"

"YouTube videos," he offered, humbly. I liked him more every second. "Come here," he said.

He was standing in the first part of the room which was sectioned off as a little kitchen and eating area. I leaned my back against the counter and he came to stand in front of me. "So, what are the rules?" he asked.

INVITATION

"Rules?"

"Yeah, well, I know you are worried about where we go from here. We should probably talk about the plan."

I laughed a little at the idea of the plan, but I loved it too. "I won't let myself get too attached to you," I blurted out before I could really filter it.

"We'll see." He leaned in towards me. I leaned back. "No, I mean it. I can't. I do like you. I would really like to kiss you again, but..."

"Okay, I understand. I guess this is every guy's dream, right? Gorgeous woman wants sex with no strings attached?" I looked at him sharply. "Sorry, shouldn't have said sex. Yet." As he said it his body pushed harder against mine and mine pushed back. My lips were so close to his I could feel his breath.

"I'm not saying no for sure. I just don't know how it will go. I need to try and see..."

"So, I', an experiment?"

I opened my mouth to disagree, but he was laughing. "I like it! I get it. You need to have control and you need to be with someone who will stop exactly when you need him to?"

I was flooded with relief. "Yes! Yes!" I was so excited that he understood.

"Okay," he leaned away from me, folding his arms across his chest. "You start."

At first it seemed ridiculous and I just stood there. But after a few seconds, the irresistible force of our attraction took over. My body softened, readying itself for new possibilities.

Beside the kitchen was a small living room, and I pulled Liam toward the sofa. We sat down beside each other. He put his hands to his sides and looked straight ahead. "Okay," he said. "Try to seduce me. But be warned. I'm slow to warm up."

We both looked at the growing bulge in his pants and laughed. He put his arm around me, moved close to me face and waited. My lips tingled, desperate for contact. I moved my face towards his until our lips nearly touched. I pulled back a bit, teasing us both, then leaned in again. Finally, I put my hands in his hair, pulling him to me.

Our lips touched gently. He groaned, a sexy desperate noise that made me feel wanted and powerful. Soon we were kissing with our whole bodies, limbs entwined, clutching to being each other even closer.

The angle of our bodies on the couch was awkward, so I moved to straddle him. I was so swollen and wet that as we kissed my hips started moving on their own. His hips rose to meet mine. I was losing control. I needed to slow down.

I got off his lap and kneeled down in front of him. "You okay?" he asked, concerned. I rested my cheek against the inside of his thigh.

"Yes, yes, I'm amazing. This is amazing." I tried to slow my breathing. "It's just, it's almost too much, you know? Can we just concentrate on you for a minute?" He leaned back and almost growled.

"Oh my god, woman. This is a dream, it has to be."

I smiled up at him. "So hands at your sides, and no touching."

He clenched his fists and pinned them to his sides. I was suddenly unsure of what to do. I was 23, but I had never really explored a man's body. Not without him instantly being inside me and the whole thing being over before I knew what had happened. Now suddenly the most delicious specimen I had ever seen was in front of me and I could do whatever I wanted. And, best of all, I could stop if I needed to.

I spread his knees apart and moved between them. I looked nervously at the door. "I'm worried someone's going to barge in."

He laughed, and it sounded a little bitter. "My parents aren't home. They're never home. And I'm the only one with the key, anyway." He held my hands, helping me up off the floor. "But let's go over here." He pulled me towards the far end of the room. Hidden behind a wall was a modern and masculine platform bed. He sat down on it and tried to pull me down beside him.

"No," I smiled. I stood in front of him. He's a tall man, six feet at least, and I'm about five feet six inches, so as I stood in front of him, my mouth was at the top of his head. I kissed him there. He smelled amazing. I kissed the sides of his face and his mouth. I started to undo his shirt, and he groaned again.

He leaned back, closing his eyes. I unbuttoned him all the way then pushed the shirt off his muscular shoulders. I wanted to take a lot of time, to kiss him everywhere, but there was an urgency to his moans that drew me downward.

I kissed his collarbones and his chest. Then I put my tongue on his stomach and worked my way down to the edge of his pants. His head was shaking back and forth, and he moaned, "Oh, Madison, I want you. Oh, my god. I want you."

But he couldn't have me. Even though I was so swollen and throbbing and all I could think about was ripping my clothes off and riding him until we both screamed, it wasn't time. I wasn't ready.

But he was ready, and that gave me so much pleasure. "Stand up," I ordered him. He did as I asked and stood in front of me.

"Please let me touch you. I have to touch you." I shook my head and ran my hands down the front of his chest and then his abdomen. I brushed my hand against his groin, and his hard-on pounded against his pants under my touch. I undid his button and then his zipper, rubbing a little harder against him as I made my way down. I pushed him back onto the bed and pulled off the rest of his clothing.

He was naked in front of me and he was gorgeous. I moved up the side of the bed a bit and patted the pillow. "Lie down". He did and I sat down beside him. I ran my fingers down his abdomen. Then I started at his feet and ran my fingers more roughly up the inner surfaces of his legs. I massaged and licked his upper thighs.

Liam's hands were clenching, trying not to grab for me. I moved his legs apart and kneeled between them. I stroked his abdomen, coming closer and closer to his shaft. I was timid and nervous. I wasn't sure I was any good at this particular maneuver. But I was so turned on, and so attracted to him that I wanted to lick and nibble and bite him. I wanted him pulling me down on him. I wanted to hear him cry out.

In the half-light of his bedroom, I saw the most beautiful body. It was all mine to play with, but I could feel that it was getting too intense for both of us. His hands had found their way to my hair and he was trying to pull me up toward his face. I knew that if my breasts felt his chest beneath me, if my swollen cleft pressed down on him, I would be beyond control.

So instead, I ran a finger lightly up his shaft, which throbbed, hard and swollen. The skin was taut and soft and hot. I bent down to lick his balls in figure-eight movements until he began crying out, "Oh god, Madison. Please, please, please." I put my left hand where my tongue had been, and massaged him gently. I teased his cock with my tongue. I circled the tip once, then twice, and then took his whole shaft into my mouth.

He gasped and moaned. He grabbed my hair and pulled me onto him. I could have teased him a little more, but he had had enough. His hands ran wildly through my hair. It was time to let him go. I moved my mouth slowly at first, increasing the pulling sensation, rubbing his tenderest area with my tongue: then faster and faster until he was moaning incoherently, his hips bucking.

God I wanted him to be pounding into me. The thought was both shocking and delicious. I was nowhere near ready for that kind of intimacy and loss of control. It had to wait. Faster and faster I went until his whole body tensed and he screamed my name again and again. The spasms lasted a long time. As his body relaxed and his breathing sowed, he stroked my hair and sighed contentedly.

Eventually, I made my way up his body, kissing as I went. He was still off in another place, pleasure land, you know? I felt so good. I didn't feel frightened or used or dirty. I felt powerful and sexy.

I lay down fully clothed beside his naked body, and kissed the side of his face. I felt him smiling, so I kissed his lips very gently many times. Then I lay down beside him and we both fell asleep.

CHAPTER SIX

I sat up suddenly in Liam's bed and searched for a clock: 4am. We weren't late for work, thank god. I hadn't exactly been making the best of impressions with my team and I needed to make up for it. I leaned back in bed and looked over at Liam. I guess I was supposed to feel remorse, or something, but I felt pretty good. Really good, actually. Until I remembered Chloe.

I jumped out of bed, searching in the darkness for my phone. I had put the ringer on silent, for obvious reasons. When I looked at the screen, I saw that Chloe had texted me eleven times and left six phone messages.

I had let her know the afternoon before that I was going to meet up with Liam, but I hadn't talked to her since. She was obviously worried; she saw clearly freaking out.

I was a coward and decided to text her back instead of calling, but she called back right away. "Where the hell have you been?" She yelled. "Are you okay?"

I tried to assure that I was fine, but she was too angry to listen. "How could you just disappear like that? You can't do this stuff. I almost called your father."

"Jesus, Chloe, don't you ever call him." I snapped.

"It was him or the police. I thought it was happening again. I can't believe you didn't think to call." She stuttered a bit, like she was trying to put together her next words. "Screw you!" she hollered and then hung up.

I looked over at Liam still in bed, his head resting on an elbow. "Wow, I heard that 'screw you' from over here. Who was that?"

"Chloe, my roommate. My friend."

"She's kind of intense," he laughed nervously.

"No, she's great. She was really there for me when...you know. She feels guilty because she left me alone that night at the bar with Brandon. She was just scared because I didn't call. It was a jerk thing for me to do."

"Come here, little jerk," he said and in spite of feeling guilty as hell, I wandered over to him and curled back into the blankets. "Do you want to try to sleep some more?"

"Yes," I answered. "But I won't. I'm up now."

"Me too. Let's eat and then I'll drop you at your place in time for work. I don't think I have anything edible around here, so let's go out."

I left the bed and headed into the bathroom. I scrubbed my teeth with some toothpaste and splashed cold water on my face. My awful clothes and boring hair suddenly depressed me. There wasn't much I could do about it right then, though.

I left the washroom and found Liam already at the front door, dressed in his coat and boots, ready to go. It could have been that he was really hungry, but I felt like he was trying to hustle me out of the room, maybe out of his life.

As I reached to put my coat on, he pulled me in for a kiss. He gazed down at me while his thumb stroked my cheek. "You are so beautiful." He smiled and kissed me again.

I drew back. "Stop saying that, okay? I know it isn't true, and it feels like you're making fun of me." I looked away because my voice had cracked and I was afraid I'd cry.

He looked so confused. "What are you talking about? You're amazing. Your face is perfect. No man could look at your lips and not want to kiss them. Or bite them. And when that gorgeous hair fell all over me – it looks like gold for god's sake -- I thought I would come right then."

I felt like an idiot. Was I always going to feel bad about myself? Was I always going to think men were just dirt bags trying to use women? "I'm sorry," I offered. "You must think I'm just another screwed-up mess. If this is a big hassle, I totally get it. We can just leave this as it is." I picked up my phone and started dialing. "I'll take a cab home."

Liam took my phone, put it into my bag, and pulled me towards him. "Like hell. I owe you some fun and it's going to happen." He started kissing me, pushing me back toward the bed. I was smiling, but nothing was going to happen. "I have to be on time today. I have to go."

"Oh, me too," he sighed. "I was just trying to be spontaneous and irresponsible for once."

We walked to the car. We both seemed pretty comfortable, but there was still an awkward conversation ahead of us. He pulled out onto the road.

"So," he started. "Last night was totally amazing. Do you think you might keep me around for a while?"

"Well, it's possible," I said. "But I still can't guarantee you anything. Maybe you don't want the trouble?"

"I'll take my chances."

We drove the rest of the way to the diner in contented silence. It was insanely early and we were both tired. At the diner we ate huge stacks of pancakes. We hardly spoke, but the silences were comfortable. He was easy to be with.

When we had finished eating, and Liam had had three cups of coffee, we got back in the car. I gave him directions to my apartment and he dropped me by the front door.

"I think I should walk you in," he offered.

"That would be great," I started getting out of the car, "but Chloe will likely tear into me, and you don't need to start your day with that."

He tapped his fingers against the steering wheel and stared straight ahead. "So how about we skip the whole 'will he, won't she call, text, email?', crap and just say we'll see each other again."

I guess I could have found him arrogant and presumptuous. This was no Victorian courtship. But he seemed kind, and mature enough to get why I was sort of screwed up. He was so straightforward and honest.

INVITATION

"Okay, that would be great."

"Tonight?"

I laughed at his enthusiasm. "No, I'm on call." We compared schedules and realized that one or the other of us would be on call for the next four nights, so we agreed we'd meet up on the fifth.

CHAPTER SEVEN

It was a long time to have to wait to see him, but the days went by. As students, we started work at 7am and ended at 6pm, unless we were on call. If that was the case, then we stayed at the hospital all night and all of the next day as well. I loved seeing the kids, and I tried to block the thoughts of Liam out. But even though my mind could ignore him, my body couldn't.

A couple of times I saw him from a distance in the hospital. My reaction surprised me every time. I felt like I was having a dozen tiny orgasms. I worried about how far I might let myself go when we did meet up again, but I wasn't worried enough to cancel the date.

Little Mario Andretti, Alex, was in for a round of chemo. He had a type of leukemia that was supposed to respond well to treatment, but he wasn't improving much. He seemed a little sicker the next time I saw him. Within three days he was too sick to race around in his chair.

I had a few extra minutes after rounds, so I helped him get out of bed and into his wheelchair, and headed out the door.

"Dr. Spencer!"

I turned to see my boss, Dr. Olsen, coming at me, looking furious.

"This patient is immunocompromised! He can't wander around the hospital picking up viruses and bacteria!" She looked at me as though I was a moron, which was fair, because that was a pretty stupid thing to do. There was just so much to learn.

So, I put him back to bed and went downstairs to the gift shop. I was in luck; in-between the birth announcements and the flowers I found a box of toy cars. I took them back up to Alex's room. This time I put on a mask before I went in.

"Close your eyes, kiddo."

"Forget it. That's what they say right before they do something that hurts."

This working with sick kids was going to take some getting used to. He was only six, yet he was completely unafraid of telling adults off. He'd spent too much time in hospitals. "Okay," I sat on the edge of his bed. "Fair enough. I brought you something." I handed him the package of cars.

A giant smile burst across his face. He tried to open the package, but was too weak. I opened them for him. He started building a make-believe highway on his sheets right away.

Suddenly Dr. Olsen reappeared. "Alex, where did you get those? Have they been cleaned?" Alex pointed at me and shrugged.

"They're new," I responded. "But I can wash them off anyway. Just in case."

"Do that", the doctor snapped at me. "Then finish rounding please. We need you in radiology for a tutorial."

When she left, I looked back at Alex.

"Sorry I keep getting you in trouble," he said. "I really love the cars."

"Oh, don't worry about it. I'm pretty much always in trouble." He gave me a huge grin, which made getting into trouble almost worth it.

I say it was "almost" worth it because the woman did still hold my future in her hands. Medical school is no place for independent thinkers or rebels, and I'd have to start convincing her I wasn't some lazy, brainless flake.

As I left Alex's room and turned the corner, I ran right into the tall blond guy from orientation. He was so close to the door that I wondered if he had been eavesdropping.

"Boy, she sure doesn't like you," he said to me.

I didn't understand. "Excuse me? Who?"

"Dr. Olsen. It's rough if she decides not to like you. She'll be on your case like crazy for the next three months for sure."

I was taken aback. I hadn't really done anything so bad. Not bad enough to doom me for the next three months. Had I? It suddenly occurred to me that I didn't even know this guy's name.

"I'm sorry. I know we met the other day, but I'm bad with names..."

His face clouded over with anger. He was obviously not used to people forgetting about him. Just that morning I had been warned about his temper and told that he slept around a lot; but since I had once been almost destroyed by rumors, I refused to listen to them. His smarmy manner was making me wonder, though.

"I'm Owen. And I can help you out with Olsen." He leaned too close to me and I took a step back. Once again he seemed really annoyed.

"What do you mean? How?" I felt a powerful urge to get away from the guy, but I was trapped. He was a senior resident, so eventually, somewhere along the way, we would be on the same rotation and he would be in charge of me. If what he said was true, and I was off to a rough start, then I needed to make more friends and fewer enemies.

"She likes me, and I can put in a good word for you." He leaned against the wall as though we were having a casual conversation, but I suddenly felt a little nauseated.

"But you don't even know me."

"Well," he put his hand on my shoulder. "Things can change." I stood very still, wanting to slap his hand off me, but very aware of the trouble this guy could cause.

"Okay," I laughed nervously as I moved away from him. "Well, sure, I guess." I took a few steps away. "I've got to get downstairs." I practically ran away from him. On my way past the nursing desk I thought I saw the head nurse give me a sympathetic look. My life had gone from nothing happening to too much happening in such a short time.

CHAPTER EIGHT

After work, I was at home tidying up when Chloe arrived. She threw he bag on the floor and melted into the couch. "Is it just me, or is being a medical interns probably going to kill us?"

I laughed, but nodded in agreement. "God, I know. It's only been a week, but I've already been on call three times and I'm so tired that during the day I fantasize about pillows and blankets, and going to sleep." There may have been one or two other fantasies in there, but never mind.

Chloe sat up. "Me too. Hey, you wanna do something tomorrow night if we're not both dead?"

I had been dreading this conversation, but it had to happen.

"I think I'm going out tomorrow. With Liam." Chloe's face shifted rapidly from surprise to disgust. "What?" I asked defensively. "He's a nice guy. I can't stay afraid forever."

I sat down beside her on the couch but she got up to pace in front of me.

"We've talked about this so many times." She glared at me and threw up her arms. "Last time nearly destroyed you. Life is stressful enough right now. You've got to concentrate on school."

Chloe really had been so good to me, but I was suddenly tired of the lectures. "Chloe, it's been two years. For two years I've been a shell of a person. I'm afraid of everything." I picked up the edge of my shirt and flipped it away from me. "I dress like a bag lady."

"No, you don't."

"Give me a break."

"But you've been safe." She said this like it was the end of the discussion. I was starting to see that Chloe treated me too much like a child.

"Yes, I've been safe, but I have been lonely!" She looked at me, offended. "Don't even start with that. You know exactly what I mean. I miss being touched. I miss using my body for fun things, not to just get through the day. I don't want to spend the rest of my life just surviving!"

"He'll break your heart. They always do."

"Who are these 'they's'? I had a couple of sweet boyfriends in high school, and then asshole Brandon. One jerk who hurt me."

"A whole bunch of jerks hurt you."

"But Brandon was behind it." She conceded the point. A bunch of guys had been involved, but I could only be blamed for my terrible choice of one of them.

"Liam could be the same. These medical guys are all assholes. They're loser nerds until they put on a lab coat, then every female, or male depending on sexual affiliation, in the hospital is falling all over them. They go all insta-arrogant."

I laughed. "Not quite. Plus there are plenty of asshole female doctors, too." I could see she was considering some of our classmates. She smiled a bit, but it was a sad smile. "He'll bring you down."

"No, he won't. He can't."

"What do you mean?"

"We talked about it. No love, no big commitment. No hearts and balloons and violins in the background."

"You talked about it? How do two strangers sit down and just start talking about this?"

So, I explained to Chloe about the coffee shop disaster and how I had told Liam some of the stuff about The Incident. I told her how easy it was to talk to him.

"But," she interrupted. "You told him about what happened to you and his plan was to not be nice to you, but just to have sex?!"

When she put it that way it didn't sound great. "No, that's not it."

"Whatever." She was pissed now. Chloe was really good at giving advice, but she turned pretty ugly if you didn't follow it.

"Chloe, listen. Everyone has either treated me like disgusting damaged goods, or like some pathetic victim that needs to be locked away and kept safe. He is the first person who has ever heard about it and been nice about it, and then just treated me like an adult." I really wanted her to understand. "I feel healthy with him, and powerful and sexy, in a really good way."

"Oh Maddie, he's just using you. This is so fucked up."

"It's not fucked up. He is being nice to me by treating me like a whole, desirable woman. Being with him physically is amazing. He is nice to me AND we get physical. It doesn't have to be one or the other."

"I can't believe you're having sex with this stranger."

"We're not having sex. There are a lot of rules. I'm in charge."

"Oh, bullshit. This is all bullshit, because you WILL get hurt."

"No I won't. No love, just fun."

"Oh, seriously, come on. You probably love him already." She stormed out of the room and slammed the door.

I appreciated her concern, I really did, but it was becoming too much. She was turning into my father, and I had left that scene behind a long time ago. I really hoped we were going to be able to work this out. I didn't think we'd be able to stay friends and roommates if she was going to live in the past. It didn't feel right that she was so angry with me for trying to move on in a healthy way.

CHAPTER NINE

Friday evening came at last, and I tried to push all of Chloe's negativity out of my head.

Liam and I met again by his car. We were both exhausted and hungry, but I perked up completely when I saw him. I couldn't even begin to play hard to get. This man knew I wanted him. I was playing the game all wrong, and so far I was having the time of my life.

We agreed on a local vegetarian restaurant. He said he loved the pizza there. I was willing to try anything as long as it didn't make my breath smell awful. I got butternut squash soup and a grilled cheese sandwich. Of course the names of the items were long and complicated, and there was some kind of exotic goat cheese from the island of something or other. But at heart it was just warm comfort food. The best kind of meal for a romantic, or at least a physically exciting, rendezvous on a rainy evening in Seattle. Easy to digest and no garlic! It was a winner all around.

We ate and chatted about work. When we had finished eating, we passed on coffee and dessert, eager to get going.

We went back outside. The rain was torrential once more, so we hustled into the car. I love driving in the rain. I feel cozy and safe, and I love the shoop shoop of the windshield wipers. We were both relaxed and comfortable and didn't talk much on the drive. I wished Chloe could see how it really was. It was so easy to be comfortable around him. I hadn't thought I would ever feel comfortable around another man, and here I was. It seemed like something to celebrate, and I was determined to keep ahold of my new optimism.

Eventually we ended up back at the peaceful pseudo-apartment beside his parents' house. It seemed like a long drive for him, to and from the hospital, but I was beginning to understand how nice it was to feel like we were really getting away from there. The change in geography definitely helped us to leave the stresses of work behind.

I hadn't been sure how to prepare for this visit. I had brought a toothbrush and some extra clothes. At work I'd taken a quick shower so I could smell like soap instead of the hospital. I had even shaved. Just my lower legs and underarms. No, that's not true. I had shaved nearly everywhere.

As we pulled to a stop, Liam looked over at me. "I should have asked if this was okay." He signaled the area around us with his hands. For the first time that evening, he looked a little nervous. "I mean, we could go to the movies or something. Hang out at your place."

The thought of us hanging out with Chloe made me laugh. "No, I like all your parts right where they are. Chloe would probably try to cut something off." Liam looked alarmed. I smiled at him, but didn't go into the details. I didn't want any of the past there with me.

I got out of the car. "And I'm the one who said no romance, no dates, no love crap." He looked a little stunned. "Too harsh?" I asked.

"No, Madison. At least I don't think so. I'm trying to decide if this is the best thing to ever happen, or if I'm going to really regret it."

I really doubted that he was going to regret it.

When we got into his room, we sat down on the sofa, hands in our laps, backs straight. "So," Liam started...

It was strange sitting there about to negotiate the night's festivities. But I was also finding it insanely arousing. We had been apart five days and every extra second was just increasing the crazy sexual tension.

I started with, "I enjoyed last time. We could start there." We both laughed a little at the formality of my speech.

He moved closer, pinning me against the arm of the sofa. "I enjoyed last time, too. But this time it's my turn to play."

"Okay," I pretended to still be calm and rational, but I could barely breathe. The man made my body writhe with pleasure just looking at him. "But I have to keep my clothes on. Maybe not all of them, but some. Okay? That has to be okay."

He looked me over. I was wearing a t-shirt and a long skirt. He put his hand up under the hem of my skirt and grazed his fingers along my outer thigh. He touched my ass lightly. It sent tingles all down my body, and in-between my legs. My mouth was already open, panting a bit. "I think that will allow me access to the areas I need. So, agreed."

He scooped me up like I was light as a feather and carried me to his bed. He fluffed up the pillows and laid me back against them. But I sat straight back up and turned off the light.

"It can't be like last time. I can't just be the whole center of attention. It's too embarrassing."

"Was I supposed to be embarrassed last time? Because I felt a lot of things, and embarrassed isn't one of them."

"Okay. Point taken. But I want to be able to, you know, respond if, you know, that seems like something I might want to do."

He lay down on his side, facing me. His lips were brushing against mine. He touched his tongue to my upper lip and then bit the lower one gently. His voice was hoarse with desire. "I can't talk about this anymore."

I started kissing him back and we were soon lost in each other. My lips were swollen and on fire. His tongue teased my lips open wider and then plunged in. Our tongues moved together, making each other crazy with excitement.

My body wrapped around him. His arms moved up and down my back, sending shocks of electricity to my breasts and my center. Every time he touched me the feelings intensified. Soon I was almost dizzy with lust.

He grabbed my ass, pushing my pussy against him. We were still fully clothed, but I could feel him throbbing. The pressure against me felt amazing. My breathing was heavy and my heart pounded.

He rolled me onto my back and lay down on top of me gently. His hand moved forward onto my breast, and he cupped it tenderly. Sparks of pleasure flew through my body. He put his hand under my shirt, onto my stomach. Then he lowered his face to my stomach, and kissed me over and over again, moving closer to the edge of my skirt.

"I need a minute," Liam said. I didn't think I could wait. I put my hands in his luscious hair and held his face to my belly. I didn't push him downward, but God I wanted to. All I could think about was being sucked and licked by that beautiful mouth.

Liam's breathing slowed a little, and he kissed my stomach again. This time when he moved lower, but I held his face and pulled it towards me. It turns out despite the overwhelming feeling of lust, I wasn't ready for anything so intimate. "Come up here and kiss me. I need you here." He understood.

We kissed slowly and intensely. Our mouths opened wide. Our tongues entwined. He sat up and ran his hands down my long skirt. Even through the fabric his fingers felt like fire. I was writhing with pleasure.

Then he put a hand under the hem, and started stroking my skin. "Your legs are so beautiful. You have the softest skin." As he talked, his hand reached higher and higher. I couldn't even answer him. My eyes were closed, my lips parted.

I pulled his face up to mine and pressed my cheek against his. I wanted to smell his neck and his hair. I rubbed the front of his pants, but he held my wrist still. "Please," Liam said. "Let me give you something first."

I knew I could trust him not to push for intercourse, or even oral sex. He kissed me all along my neck and whispered, "You are really, really lucky I'm so good with my fingers."

He moved his head down and gently bit my hard nipple through the thin t-shirt. I inhaled sharply. At the same time, his hand which had been stroking my inner thighs the whole time, suddenly pushed up against the wet fabric of my panties.

He stroked along my cleft gently up and down until my hips were rising to meet him. Then he put his hand down the front of my panties and starting pushing them off. I lifted my hips to let him, and felt him smile. I lifted my feet one by one to get the panties off. He pulled the skirt all the way up until I felt the cool air on my pussy. He started stroking the skin beside my cleft. I was in another world. "Oh god. Oh my god." I wanted to grab his hand and buck against it, but I made myself lie still.

My legs were still tight together, and he put a hand on either thigh and moved them slightly apart. Then he spread my lower lips apart with his left hand, leaving me exposed to the air. "Spread your legs wider for me." I should have felt embarrassed, but nothing could stop me by that point. With my outer lips still spread, he began touching the inner lips of my pussy. "You're so swollen. And so wet. Oh my god it's sexy." My body was moving on its own by then. Waves of pleasure were building in me and I pushed my swollen throbbing pussy harder against his hand. He circled around and around my sweetest spot but wouldn't touch it. I was close to begging.

He put his fingers inside me and moved them in and out. His left hand let go of my outer lips and he came back up to the pillows to kiss me more. As he did, his right hand, which had been moving inside me, slid up to my clitoris and stroked in soft slow circles. The pleasure was magical. I wanted it to last forever, but my body was climbing, begging for release.

"Faster," I practically sobbed. "Oh god, please don't stop. Please don't stop. I'm so close." His rubbing increased in pressure and speed and soon my head was whipping side to side against the pillows, and my hands were all over him, pulling him closer. I kissed him harder and harder until I had to pull away to scream out. The waves pounded out from the center of me.

He continued to stroke me very gently, and the waves kept coming and coming. I moaned and started kissing him again, but I was too weak to move anything more than that.

I was on still throbbing, still on fire. "Again?" he teased and started moving in tiny soft circles around my clitoris. It was only seconds before my hips were writhing against him again and I was crying out again. "Liam, oh god, Liam." I held on tightly to him as the orgasm ripped through me. I lay shuddering for a long time before I could breathe normally.

He kissed me and smiled down at me. He looked pleased with himself, and rightly so. "Sweet, sweet Madison. That was just my fingers. Wait 'til you see what I can do with my mouth."

I put my hand on his hot, hard penis. He lifted my hand to my mouth so I could lick it, then put it back down on him. I had planned a long, luscious sucking and licking for him, but he wrapped his hand around mine and moved them up and down his shaft. In seconds, he was coming. A wild almost painful groaning came from deep within him. He wrapped a hand through my hair and pulled my lips against his, hard.

He was sweet, to be sure, but he was definitely a man. I had no doubt that he was going to take me to amazing places and then get what he needed too. I loved the sense of barely-controlled power that radiated from him when he was coming.

CHAPTER TEN

By some miracle, we both had Saturday morning off, so we were able to sleep in a bit. I was lying in bed thinking how strange it was that I felt so comfortable there with Liam. I was remembering the events of the previous night.

The memories aroused me, but they were slightly embarrassing, too. It's so much easier to be vulnerable and open in the middle of the night. The next morning is tricky. Especially when you're not even sure what you're doing or what you mean to each other. It wasn't like a one night stand with some guy you pick up in a bar. Not that I'd ever had one. But in the movies the people leave in the middle of the night, or sneak out in the morning.

The fact that we were so comfortable together made the mornings a lot easier than that, but still, we weren't a couple, so we weren't expecting to hang out all day, right? I could see the value of all our rules, but I could also see how there might come a time when this all got really complicated.

Liam was awake too, and rolled toward me. "Feeling ok?" he asked.

"I feel better than I have in a very long time, and I think you know it." I gave his well-built chest a quick kiss. I got out of bed and headed for the bathroom. I did the early morning bathroom necessities, particularly the tooth brushing.

His apartment was freezing, so I was shivering by the time I made it back to bed. I pushed on his shoulder and flipped him over onto his back. I didn't know the morning rules, but I figured I could make some of my own. I reached under the blanket and found him hard and long. He moaned as I touched him. "I'm sorry you didn't get to have enough attention last night", I teased. "I can't believe I just fell asleep. Well, more like passed out. That was intense."

He grinned. "Yeah, that was definitely fun."

"But here you are. All unsatisfied." I started rubbing him, stroking up and down his shaft. He reached for me, trying to pull my t-shirt off.

I froze. I suddenly felt like bursting into tears. "I'm so sorry. I'm a mess." I tried to lighten the mood a little. "They're going to kick me off Pediatrics and send me to Psychiatry." We both laughed lightly. He lifted my hand to his face and started kissing my inner arm.

"I think you're amazing," he said. "I love that you're here with me. I think you're brave."

The conversation was getting a little heavy for a Saturday morning. I was relieved when his tone turned flirtatious again "You don't owe me an orgasm. We're not keeping score." He paused, considering. "Well," he joked, "I'm sort of keeping score. But I like when you're in the lead. It proves I'm extremely manly." Just like uncomfortable tension was gone. I smiled and relaxed into his embrace.

I lay there breathing in the delicious smell of him, feeling his muscular shoulders and chest. I realized that he was likely the sexiest and kindest guy I had ever run across and that if I was ever going to get over my past and all that pain, it was going to be with this man. I couldn't lose him. Whatever this was, I had to keep it.

I wanted more nights like the previous night. I realized I wanted to have sex with him, probably frequently, and I had to figure out how to get myself to that point without freaking out. I had to push my boundaries a little.

We started kissing and I made my way down to where he was swollen and hot. I gave him a long lick from his balls to his tip. He shuddered and grabbed for my head. I licked him over and over until his hips were rising up. I massaged his balls and when I stopped, he grabbed my hand and put it lower on the soft skin underneath them. "Press there," he moaned and gasped as I did. I put my mouth around him and took him in again and again. His hips rocked and he moaned.

"Wait." I stopped, and looked up at him.

"I want to look at you."

I didn't understand at first, until I saw he was tugging gently on the hem of my t-shirt. I was frightened. I hadn't been naked for anyone since the bad night. "I need to keep my underwear on."

"Stand up," he told me and I did. He propped himself up on the pillows and looked at me standing beside the bed. "I won't touch you. But I want you to take off your skirt." I stood paralyzed for a minute realizing that I wanted to be with this man. I wanted to please him, and I wanted to please myself. It was time.

The light in the room was dim which gave me confidence. My skirt had an elastic waist and was easy to slide down. I pushed it down past my hips and it dropped to the ground with a rustle.

I was in my white lace panties and my t-shirt. The cool air soon made my nipples hard and they pushed against my thin bra. I knew he could see them. "This is the sexiest thing I have ever seen." I blushed and looked at the floor.

"No, look at me." I did. "Keep looking at me and take off your shirt." My heart was pounding and my chest was heaving with fear, but I needed to do it.

I pulled my shirt over my head quickly and tossed it onto the floor. I turned back to look into his eyes once again. "Oh, my god," he said. "Look at you. I want to touch you everywhere. I want to lick every tiny part of you."

I felt braver than I ever had. He was looking at me the way you would look at a beautiful painting. It was nothing like my ex-boyfriend or those animals at the bar had looked at me. It wasn't love, we had agreed on that, but it was like he loved my body. And being with someone who was so openly adoring me gave me strength. He hadn't asked, but I reached behind me to unfasten my bra. I took it off and stood trembling in front of him.

He shook his head in disbelief. "How is this happening? How is this gorgeous woman standing beside my bed?"

He sat up on the edge of the bed. He held his hands out for me to take, if I wanted. Of course I did. He pulled me towards him and kissed my lips. He kissed my neck and my shoulders until electricity was buzzing along my entire body.

He kissed my nipple. "You have the most beautiful breasts I've ever seen. Your whole body, your whole body is insane." My back arched in pleasure, pushing my breast deeper into his mouth. I stayed motionless as he licked and lightly bit my nipples. I wrapped my fingers in his hair to pull him closer, and to steady myself. My legs were so weak I could barely stand. I dropped down onto my knees to lick his shaft again.

He leaned back to watch. He was close. He closed his eyes and his head dipped back. He thrust up into my mouth and I took as much as I could again and again. I squeezed his balls gently and it pushed him over the edge. He grabbed my head and came hard. Yelling out with a pleasure so intense it sounded almost like pain.

The spasms were powerful and long lasting. Eventually, he flopped onto his back, completely sated and relaxed. Once he was breathing normally again, he whispered, "Come here. It's time I showed you what my mouth can do."

I climbed up towards him, my knees on either side of his waist. He pulled me down to him until my breast was in his mouth. He flicked my nipples with his tongue until I was gasping.

I was hot and swollen. My panties were sopping. He put his hand on my mound, pushing a finger along my cleft and I cried out. I was ready for him. I was so ready.

Suddenly he stopped. "Did you hear that?" He focused on some sound I had not heard. Then we heard footsteps. "Oh, you have got to be kidding me." He shook his head in disgust.

Someone was banging on his door. "Honey? Honey? I know you're in there. I can see your car."

I froze. "I haven't seen my mother for three months, and she shows up now. Jesus Christ."

He rolled out from under me and got up. He jumped into a pair of pants, zipped up quickly, and stormed around the wall that hid the bed.

I heard him open the door. I curled myself into a tiny ball and hid under the sheets. I was terrified that she'd come in and see me. I was terrified that she would see me and call me a slut. I started to hyperventilate.

CHAPTER ELEVEN

Liam somehow got rid of his mother and came back to bed. I tried to relax, but he must have seen something in my eyes. "What's wrong?"

"I don't know," I answered. "Nothing, really. I was just afraid she was going to come in here and see me naked and start yelling." My voice broke. The lump in my throat made it hard to swallow.

I got up and started to get dressed. Liam grabbed a shirt. "You could stay a while," he offered, but we both knew that the moment had passed. We couldn't be intimate with the threat of his mother's return looming over us, and we weren't a real couple who could make scrambled eggs and read the paper. Or whatever it is mature people are supposed to do.

"No, I'll go."

"We'll both go. I'm starved." I smiled to myself. When was this guy ever not starved?

"But first," he pulled me to the sofa, and sat us both down. "Why did you think my mother would start yelling"? He chuckled, but I didn't think anything was very funny. "She would just freeze and then back up really slowly on her high heels, and we would all pretend it never happened."

"I bet."

"No, seriously. What's this about?"

"Are you sure you want to deal with this right now?"

"We're already dealing with this right now. You might as well tell me the story."

I flopped back against the sofa. I had been so determined to just have some fun. Why was this coming up? And why did I have to ruin a great morning with all my crap?

"Okay, but I'm going to make it really short."

"Fine. Go."

"I broke up with a guy, Brandon. We were in youth group together for a while. Don't laugh." He was laughing. "It's not actually that funny. My father is a minister."

Liam started choking. "Holy shit! Is he going to come after me?"

"No, he doesn't talk to me. That's not a concern." I sighed. This stuff made me so tired. "So Brandon wanted to stay virgins until we got married."

"Then why the fuck did he date the most desirable girl in the universe?"

"Stop interrupting. But thank you."

"Anyway, after a year, we 'slipped'."

"You got it on?"

"Yes."

"Was it good?"

"Shut up. No."

He crossed his arms over his chest, nodding his head and grinning smugly.

I continued. "It didn't bother me at all because, by then, I didn't believe the things my father and his church believed. But Brandon claimed to. He was distraught and I thought I loved him. So, because I was a 'fallen woman', we decided to get engaged."

"Of course. Perfectly reasonable conclusion."

"Please don't make fun of me. It seemed like life or death at the time. I pretended to go along with it because my father was head of the church; and Brandon's father is my father's best friend and right hand man."

"So, no pressure."

"Exactly."

"But this sounds like something from the 1950's!" He was incredulous.

"Wake up, Liam." I couldn't keep the bitterness out of my voice. "Plenty of people in America think this way. I just happened to be someone who felt differently who was trapped in this church."

"Sounds more like a cult."

My anger flashed. "Hey, that's my Dad you're talking about." I'm sure Liam was thinking, 'The Dad who doesn't talk to you?', but he stayed quiet.

"Sorry. It's a difficult subject." He reached for my hand and gave it a quick squeeze.

"Eventually, for many reasons, I broke up with Brandon." I took a breath. "He went a little psycho." I rubbed my face with my hands. God I hated telling this story.

"What did he do?"

"He invited me out to talk so he could have 'closure'. I actually thought I owed him that. I met him at a bar, which should have been a big clue that something was up. We never drank." I took a deep breath. "He bought me a drink, put a roofie in it, and brought it to our table. The last thing I remember about the evening was Brandon saying, 'You're just an ugly fucking slut, and soon everyone will know it."

"Oh, Madison." Liam reached over to hold me, but I moved away.

"Just let me finish because I don't think I can ever talk about this again."

"Okay." Liam held onto my hand, but leaned back to give me some space.

"He and his friends dragged me to the bathroom, took my clothes off and left me there."

"Left you?" Liam looked as though he was having a heart attack.

"Somebody wrote on me, moved me into awful positions, and took pictures. But you can't see anyone's face in the pictures.

Except mine." I tried to calm my erratic breathing. "Eventually the bartender came in, saw me, and called the police. They took me to the hospital and called Chloe and my father. I told my father what Brandon had done. He didn't believe me. He said it was evil for me to pull Brandon, this wonderful Christian boy from an upstanding family, into this disgusting mess I had made for myself."

There were tears streaming down my face, but my voice didn't crack. For the first time, the memories were making me feel angry and strong, rather than dirty and flawed. "I went home with my father and begged him to listen to me. I had been a good girl my whole life! I had just gotten into medical school! But all that mattered was that I had had sex, with a boyfriend I had had for three years!"

"Where was your Mom in all this?"

"Dead. Don't ask me to go into that now. This is all I can deal with this morning." Liam squeezed my hand again for reassurance and I went on. "My father still didn't believe me. He said Brandon had told his father and my father that we had never had sex, that he was still 'pure'."

"Fucking coward."

"He told them that bad things had happened to me that night because I was impure and easy and must have been in that bar asking for it."

"If I ever meet that guy I'll kill him. I'll kill your father, too. Couple of hypocritical assholes."

"Stop. Don't." I shook my head. "I was still living at home at the time. I thought maybe things could cool off after a couple of days and I could talk to my father again then. I thought he just wasn't thinking clearly. I understood that he was distraught about me, and also really trapped because this was his best friend's son and a hugely important family in the church."

"But you were his kid!"

"I know, but he really believed, believes, that I am ruined. At that moment, I could see how it might seem easier to sacrifice me. I was just one stupid, loose, ruined female. Accusing Brandon could have torn the whole congregation apart."

"That's not sounding like a bad thing to me."

"I know. But at the time, that was my congregation, too. I cared about it. I cared about my father. He had worked so hard. I thought he would eventually come around..." I stopped.

"So, what happened?"

"After we got home from the hospital, we were both exhausted and emotionally rung out. I wanted to leave it for the night. I wanted us both to cool down. I started to walk to my room, but he grabbed my arms and started shaking me. He said," my throat was so tight I couldn't talk or swallow. I massaged my neck and went on. "He told me that he was glad my mother was dead so she would never have to see what a disgusting whore I turned out to be. He said I had to get out of his house. He said I was contaminating it with my filth."

There was a long silence. I rubbed my hands across my face. "So, I packed a bag and left. I took what money I had out of the bank, stayed with Chloe for a while, got a student loan and -- ta da -- here I am."

Liam looked at me. We were both quiet. "Thank you for telling me." He sat awkwardly. "I don't know what to say."

Which was fine with me. There wasn't anything he could say. I already regretted telling him the whole story. I could only see it making things even more awkward between us. What were the rules in our new pretend relationship for comforting the other person after they'd bared their soul to you?

"It's okay. I'm okay." I stood up, and pulled him up to standing, too. "You don't have to say anything. It was a long time ago. Life's been working out pretty well for me lately." I wanted to get back to our lazy, sexy morning, not just to avoid the heavier topics, but because life really had been getting better. I wanted to be back in that better life as soon as possible.

53

CHAPTER TWELVE

Liam drove me back into the city. My mood had improved and I was back to just feeling great around him. I was tired of my horrible clothes and my ratty hair, and needed to start making some changes.

Liam had told me over and over again that I was gorgeous, but his eyes were obviously clouded with some kind of sex chemical. Now I wanted to look really nice for him. For the first time ever, I thought that that kind of attention could feel nice. I wanted to wear something pretty or sexy and have Liam's eyes grow wide. I wanted him to say, "Wow".

I'm not sure why my thoughts went instantly to lingerie. The underwear I had on at the time was actually all right. It was sweet and pretty, but I wanted something that would give me more confidence. If I was going to get over the next hurdle, then I would need to feel empowered, and sexy as hell.

I got Liam to drop me off at a street close to home filled with fabulous little shops and salons. I really didn't have money to spare, but this was important.

I got a quick haircut. I bought some soft sweaters and a pair of sexy jeans.

Next on the list was lingerie. Chloe could help me pick out more clothes another day. She'd love to head out for a fun girls' day out, and I probably owed her one. But I wasn't going to take her lingerie shopping. I'm not the kind of person who can prance around in front of sales people or even best friends. Thinking about a girls' day, made me realize. I was really missing Chloe.

INVITATION

She was my best friend and this amazing, wonderful thing was happening to me. I wanted to be able to tell her all about it, but I now I dreaded telling her anything. I wanted to be friends like we had been before, before the ugliness with Brandon, but she wasn't letting it happen.

I walked into the first shop with frilly things in the window and instantly knew I was in the right place. The pieces were sexy and classic. A salesperson came towards me. She had a turquoise bra with feathers in her hand, and held it up. "You like?" she asked.

"No!" I said before I could filter myself. She laughed.

"Good. Finally a young one with some taste. What are you looking for, sweetie?"

I felt like I had found my own tiny fairy godmother. Usually I push people's kindness and help away, but she was so warm and lovely. It felt wonderful to let my guard down and have her take care of me.

I gave her a condensed version of the story. "Basically, I want to feel like I look good. I think it might help me to be braver."

She nodded. "Meet me by the changing rooms." She floated through the store, gathering up a large collection of pretty things. She hung each one up in the changing room.

"Some people want me to stay in here to help them."

I tried not to look horrified. "Oh, no. Thank you, but that's all right."

She laughed as she closed the curtain up tightly behind her. "That's what I figured. I'll be back to check on you in a sec."

I tried on many things, feeling okay about each of them. Nothing really blew me away until I picked up a black lace set and put them on. They were so tiny, and seemed so plain. I wasn't expecting much, but when I looked up into the mirror I was amazed. The bikini underwear made my waist look even slimmer, and emphasized the curve of my hips.

The demi-bra barely covered my nipples. It pushed my breasts up slightly, so it would be easy for Liam to push the fabric down and take my breast into his mouth...

God, is it normal to get turned on in a lingerie dressing room? I imagined Liam touching me between the legs, and then I did it to myself, just to see how it felt. Oh my god, this was the set. I changed back into my regular clothes and made my way to the cash register. "That was quick," exclaimed the sales person. "Did you like the pink teddy?"

I put the black bra and panties on the counter. "I didn't get a chance to try that one. Next time for sure."

"Nice choice." She rang up my purchase. "I'm giving you some free samples of skin products because you're adorable, and I hope you have a great night." I was staring at the exact human opposite of my father. I wanted to give her a hug, but that was a little beyond my comfort level. Baby steps and all.

I grabbed my bag filled with sexy confidence and headed out onto the street. It was another unusually beautiful day on the rainy coast, so I took my time getting home. For the first time in two years I was smiling again and, though I wasn't exactly Mrs. Outgoing, I wasn't staring at the ground avoiding eye contact either.

The amazing smells coming from a bakery stopped me in my tracks. Everything looked beautiful and delicious. I went in and nearly swooned from the heavenly aromas. I chose a strawberry tart and sat at an outside table to eat it.

It was too cold to eat outside really, but I wanted the whole Parisian experience. Sexy new man, pretty underwear, strawberry tart, outdoor café. Check, check, check and check.

I dipped my finger into the red glaze and sucked it off. I had always done this as a child, but now the action felt illicit and sensual. I thought of Liam and the things his tongue might do.

I was so turned on again that I got up to head home. I figured I might have to take care of things myself before the throbbing drove me insane. I definitely needed some privacy. Possibly the bathtub.

INVITATION

I couldn't remember Chloe's schedule and was guiltily hoping she wouldn't be home when I got there. I was also hoping she'd be gone so I could avoid her disapproving glare. I had run out of patience with her, and was worried a big scene might be coming. I really didn't want it to happen on this particular day. It was shaping up to be one of the best days of my life so far.

CHAPTER THIRTEEN

No such luck. As soon as I walked in the door, she was on me. "Where were you? You said you'd be here by noon at the latest! It's nearly two!"

I took a deep breath, trying to control my anger, but this just had to stop. "Chloe, I have tried to explain this to you. If you don't understand, that's fine, but you've got to back off. There's having a person's back and then there's just trying to run someone else's life."

"You're messing up again, and we have to talk." She sat down and took out a piece of paper.

"I'm through talking about this, Chloe. You respect my choices or..."

"Or what?" another voice barked. It was deep and mean and terribly familiar. I turned toward the kitchen to see my father walking toward me.

I glared at Chloe. "What have you done?"

"Well," she finally looked a little sheepish. "You weren't listening to me. So I needed some help." Chloe had never really understood why I was so angry with my father. She had always just seen him as some overprotective dad. It had been a sore point between us that she had never realized how much he had hurt me.

"This is too much, Chloe. You've gone too far. I'm getting out of here." I moved quickly towards the door, but my father blocked the way.

"You're not going anywhere until you hear us out." He pulled out a piece of paper, too.

I was shaking with rage and fear. This was my apartment. It was supposed to be my safe haven. This was supposed to be my new life. Not only was Chloe doing her best to ruin my present life, she had very deliberately brought the darkness of the past right into my own home.

I stormed over to where Chloe sat on the couch, and snatched the paper out of her hand. "What is this?" I was laughing, but it was a frightening half-crazed sound. "An intervention? You're doing an intervention on me because I am trying to have some sort of life?" I threw the paper at her. "You, you, assholes...."

"Hey, you show some respect!" my father bellowed.

"Get out!" I cried. "Both of you get out."

"Madison, what you are doing is wrong," my father started in again.

"Oh, give me a break. You don't know anything about me."

"I know all about the trouble you got yourself into, and how you seem to be so stubborn and blind that you're heading down the same path again."

"I DID NOT GET MYSELF INTO TROUBLE!!!" I screamed at him.

Chloe looked afraid, and I was glad. I wanted to slam her smug face into something hard.

"Those sorts of things do not happen to decent girls. I raised you to be better than this. This is an evil life you're leading Madison and it has to end."

I knew I was going to throw up. "I am going into the bathroom, and when I come out you will both be gone."

Chloe's face went pale, my father's beet red. They both opened their mouths to talk, but I put my hand up and said in a terrifyingly dead voice, "You will both be gone."

I walked away from them into the bathroom. I locked the door, turned on the faucet, and started heaving into the toilet.

CHAPTER FOURTEEN

I knew deep down that they were wrong. If I listened to my heart and my gut I knew that the life they wanted me to live was full of fear and darkness, and what I had with Liam was light and good.

But it got to me. It brought everything back. Not just the whole awful event, but also my father's condemnation of me afterward. I had no mother, and he had never been around much, so I shouldn't have expected anything different; but if there was ever a time a parent could have done me some good, it was after the bar nightmare. A little love and support would have helped a lot; but instead he had blamed me, called me a slut, told me not to go home anymore.

I was supposed to see Liam that night, but I couldn't possibly manage it. I couldn't get out of bed. Darkness had landed on me again, and I was pinned down. I felt a million miles away from the optimistic, alive person I had been minutes before I walked into the apartment.

I texted Liam that I had to cancel. I couldn't tell him all this crap. I was screwed up, ruined, hopeless.

There would come a point where this just wouldn't be fun for him anymore and he would dump me. Or whatever it is you do to someone you're having "physical fun" with. I started to see what a bizarre game Liam and I were playing. You can't tell someone your secrets and then try to keep things casual. You can't have amazing intimacy without opening up your heart. What we were trying to do was impossible. It had to end.

INVITATION

Besides, Chloe and my father had gotten into my head. All the ugly old voices were back. I was just a slut. A stupid slut whose life was almost ruined once and who hadn't learned her lesson at all.

I stayed in bed the rest of the weekend. I put the chain on the door. I wasn't letting anyone in. I ignored the knocking and the phone calls. Fuck Chloe. She could just go back to her parents' house. She had no idea how lucky she was. She couldn't possibly know what it was like to have no one.

On Monday I went into work. I stumbled through the day, trying to stay on top of all the pages from my beeper, and the paperwork and emergencies. I didn't see Liam. I made sure I couldn't. The sight of his anger, or worse, his hurting would have pushed me over the edge.

I was barely coping at work and couldn't afford any meltdowns or screw-ups. I looked at the ground just in front of my feet when I was walked and didn't make eye contact with anyone.

I tried to pack up some of Chloe's things, but I didn't have the energy or the boxes for the job. So I called her mother. I was hoping it would go straight to messages, but, no, she picked it up. I'd known Mrs. Bayne since I was ten. She knew about most of what I had gone through.

I was expecting her to be angry with me, since I had booted Chloe out, but she sounded more confused and concerned. It almost made me cry. I longed for some good and kind-hearted mother figure to talk to. But she soon started in on how Chloe was probably right to do whatever she had done and how I had to let Chloe come back.

Of course Chloe's Mom believed in her, that was her job. That was the way things were supposed to go. Parent defends child. What the hell was wrong with my father? What the hell was wrong with me?

I had no fight left in me, so I just hung up on her. It was rude and I was ashamed, but it didn't know what else there was to do.

Her mother was wrong about a few things. The fact is, I didn't have to let Chloe come back. Only my name was on the lease. Losing my roommate would mean even more money problems, but it was worth it. I couldn't imagine ever feeling safe around Chloe again. I would text her that she had a week to move her stuff out and then I would be changing the locks. I would tell her not to show up when I was going to be at home.

She had no standing in that apartment. She had no standing in my life at all anymore.

CHAPTER FIFTEEN

At work the next day, a nurse mentioned that Dr. Humphries was looking for me.

"Who?" I asked.

She told me it was Owen, my favorite power-abusing resident. Great. Well, sure, why not? I was having that kind of week. So I had him paged and then sat down to wait. Within a couple of minutes he was leaning lounge-lizard-like against the nursing station.

"Come have coffee with me." And that's the thing with this kind of job. Because he is a senior resident, he is basically my boss. Or he could be any day. He could make the next two years of my life complete hell. He could even fail me on a rotation and mess up my whole career.

So you can never say no to these guys. Even though they treat the hospital like a bar they're trolling for dates, you have to treat them like esteemed medical professionals. It's a great set up. For them.

As we walked down the stairs to the cafeteria, he lectured me about the five symptoms to watch for in something or other, and I nodded, trying to paste an interested look on my face.

The cafeteria in our hospital is huge and Owen picked a table far from everybody else. We sat and he tapped his nails against the table. "So," he said." How are you doing?"

"You mean at work here? Great. It's great." I was so uncomfortable. I wondered how long I had to sit there to keep up the pretense of being respectful and polite. For the first time ever, I began to hope that my pager would go off.

"You look kind of down." He stopped, waiting, I guess for me to start in with my tale of woe. "If you need a friend, I'm a really good listener."

I couldn't decide whether to laugh or spit in his face. So this was the game, now. God he was creepy. Does this work on other women? Oh, I bet it does. Handsome doctor, smoothly pulling women in with his offers of compassionate listening and friendship.

So why was it I trusted Liam so much more? Liam who offered nothing but physical pleasure. Oh wait, maybe it's because this slime ball had already tried to bribe me with putting a good word into the boss who supposedly hated me. If I would date him.

But I had to keep it civil. I couldn't tell him to go to hell, much as I would have liked to. "Oh, sure, well thanks. That's a nice offer. I appreciate it, but I'm doing great. Everything is great. I'd really like to stay, but there's some lab work I need to track down before the end of the day, so I'm going to get going." I stood to leave, but he grabbed my hand.

Right at that moment I noticed Liam on the other side of the cafeteria. I had almost forgotten how handsome he was. Liam looked at me and then at my hand, which was still in Owen's grasp. His face clouded over. He put the tray he had been carrying down, and walked quickly from the room.

"I have to go," I said to Owen, and pulled my hand forcefully from his grasp. Nurses at another table had been watching us, and they started to giggle.

Owen obviously thought they were laughing at him. His body tensed and he stood. "Follow me. Now." I clenched my teeth together so hard I thought they would crack. So this was my life.

I followed Owen in silence to the area where the call rooms are. On nights when we're on call, if we're really, really lucky, there is sometimes a lull in the excitement, and we get to collapse onto one of these uncomfortable beds.

There was no way I was going into one of those rooms with Owen. He opened a door and said, "This way." I hesitated. "I want to talk to you about how you embarrassed me back there. As a physician I need to be able to maintain a level of respect in the hospital. I can't do my job if I can't command respect."

"Okay. I get it. I'm sorry. My mistake." I put my hands up and tried to back away.

He stayed planted in the open door. "Great. That's good. Let's just go in here and talk. I can give you some tips for dealing with Olsen." I had shifted my body and was moving to get away from here. To hell with my career, there was no way I was going in there.

The thing is, once you've been through something really bad, you start to wonder if you're paranoid about every future interaction. You start to wonder if you're over-reacting to situations that someone else would find normal. But even I knew that there was nothing normal about this and that he was even more than an arrogant prick. There was something really nasty going on.

I started to walk away and ran smack into Liam. Literally, I was suddenly pressed up against him. He held on to my shoulders and looked down at me. I wanted to wrap myself around him.

"Sorry about that," he said. He looked at me as if he didn't know me and walked off down the hall. He was so cold. I deserved it, but it still hurt. I watched him walking away from me and felt a terrible sadness.

Suddenly I remembered who I had been trying to get away from. I looked back to the call room to see that Owen, too, was gone. I was all alone.

CHAPTER SIXTEEN

Seeing Liam in that depressing, grungy hallway made me really understand how good he was. He glowed. He was so handsome it sometimes hurt to look at him, but it was more than that. He had goodness and decency rolling off him in waves.

I wanted to breathe him in. I wanted him to touch me, because when he touched me I felt new and clean. He had looked at me as though I were perfect. He had treated me as though I was whole, and intelligent, sexy and valuable. He was the opposite of everything Chloe and my father and Owen-the-snake were about.

I had been thinking that I ought to be able to resist him. That wanting him was a weakness, and that maybe my father was right. Maybe I was a weak woman bound for hell, or at least a life of sin and misery.

But it couldn't be true. Liam was like sunlight. He was like air. My body craved him because he was good for me. My mind craved him because he made me feel like I was a good person and that I was going to be all right. Meeting him had been the luckiest part of my life so far and I couldn't lose him. I had to talk to him. I had to try to get him back.

I figured I'd find him on one of the cardiology wards and, sure enough, after a few false starts I tracked him down. He looked up as I entered the nursing station, where we sit to write notes, and quickly looked back down again.

I sat beside him and pretended to write in a patient's chart. Neither of us wanted to look like unprofessional horny teenagers who were making dates in the hospital. But I couldn't just send him a text. I needed to be close to him when we spoke. I needed to see him. I needed him to see me, so he could really know that I was sorry, and that I wanted him.

I wrote a note and passed it to him. 'Can we talk?' Then I wrote 'YES /NO' underneath it. He did not react, and I thought he was ignoring it. My heart plummeted. I had dumped all my garbage on him and then brushed him off with a text. Then I had avoided him for a week with no explanation at all. I thought he would understand if I could just explain everything. But if he wouldn't give me that chance, then what?

I took the note back and wrote 'We can walk to my place after work. Chloe's gone'. I pushed it back again. He read it and rubbed his hands across his face. He looked tired and frustrated and torn. Who can blame him? I don't even want to deal with myself. Why would anyone else?

I took the note back once more and wrote, "I have water. Will attempt not to spill it on you. But have stocked up on baking soda, just in case."

It seemed like a century had passed since our coffee shop fiasco. I wasn't sure he'd even know what I was talking about. But I heard a quiet laugh beside me and when I looked up he was smiling. At me. It was like the sun bursting through the rain. I wanted to place my hands on the sides of his face and kiss him. He circled YES and passed it back.

"I'll be finished in half an hour," he whispered. "Meet me at the back entrance."

I hurried over to Pediatrics to check on some of my kids before I left. Alex had finished his last round of chemo and was perking up a bit. I still had to wear a mask to see him, but he seemed stronger.

"Not too long before we're back to racing in the hall, buddy." He looked up and smiled weakly. "I'm going to DE-STROY you!" he tried to yell. His voice was dry and weak.

"Geez, that sounds more like monster trucks than car racing."

"I LOVE monster trucks," he whispered as he drifted off to sleep.

I left my lab coat and stethoscope in the student lounge, grabbed my raincoat and headed out back to wait for Liam.

Half an hour passed and there was no sign of him. I started to panic. I had finally realized how good he was, how important he was to me, and it was too late. Maybe he'd had time to come to his senses. He'd probably thought about it more and decided I was too much work.

Losing him now was such a cruel trick of fate that it took my breath away. I waited ten more minutes, and then began walking home. It started to rain. I tried to hurry, but I was drenched in no time.

The rain pounded down so loudly that I didn't hear the footsteps approaching from behind. Suddenly Liam was beside me, grabbing my arm. "Hey, don't be mad. I came as soon as I could. I couldn't text you because I was talking to a patient."

I was so happy and relieved. I had no ability to play it cool. I was smiling so widely my face hurt. "I'm not mad! I thought you weren't coming. I wouldn't blame you at all."

He let go of my arm and we stood facing each other. I became aware of just how wet it was. The rain poured off our hair and eyelashes. He looked sexy as hell as the water pooled on his lips, but I was sure I looked awful.

He brushed the wet strands of hair from my forehead and stared at me. "You're so pretty in the rain." He could make everything okay so easily.

As we walked toward my apartment, I told him about Chloe and my father. "I'm not telling you this to dump it on you. I don't want you to have to deal with any of this. I just want to tell you why I disappeared for a while." He didn't say much, but he didn't turn to leave either.

CHAPTER SEVENTEEN

When we got home, we hung our soggy things up to dry and I cranked up the heat. I am always cold. On a good day I'm colder than anyone else in a room, but on a rainy dark day in March, I am cold down to my bones. I was shivering, but trying not to show it.

"Time to warm you up. Where's your bed?"

I choked out a laugh. "Wow. Even for you that's pretty bold."

"I was just going to let you get warm. Wrapping up in warm pajamas and some blankets in the best way."

I was a little embarrassed; because it turns out I was the one being a little too bold. "Okay, I'll warm up. That sounds great actually." So I took my things into the bathroom. I put my black bra and panties under my flannel pajamas. Just in case.

I found Liam already in my room, pulling the blankets down. "In you go." He tucked me in and then lay down beside me.

His face turned serious. "Why am I here?" He was asking why, after everything that had happened, did I still want him around? I wasn't sure I had all the right words I would need to explain it.

"Because I feel good when I'm with you." It was in some ways much too simple, and in some ways the whole truth. The answer was clearly acceptable, because he brought his face in close to mine.

People use the word irresistible all the time, but that is what Liam was for me. We started kissing and within a couple of seconds I was filled with heat and desire. He joined me under the blankets and our bodies twined together. His leg was between my legs, rubbing up against my core. I was desperate with need. I suddenly had to get those pajamas off. I wanted to feel him everywhere on me.

I wasn't afraid, I was on fire. I was almost ripping his clothes off. He was quickly naked. I wrapped myself around him, and moved to be on top. I felt almost, deliciously, out of control. I kissed his mouth and his neck. I bit his lips. He growled and pulled me down onto him. My pussy ached to be touched, and my hips rocked against him. He grabbed my hips and pushed himself roughly against me. He rocked slowly until my eyes were closed and my nails dug into his shoulders.

He maneuvered me onto my back and started kissing my face and my neck.

"Remember when I said I was going to kiss you all over?" he asked.

I was breathing so hard I could only whisper "Yes".

"Well, that's not going to happen right now because I can't slow this down." He clawed at my pajama top almost desperately. "I have to feel you." His fingers fumbled with the buttons, until he growled with frustration and tore the last three off. He looked down at me and moaned.

"Oh, I want this to last and last. Look at you. Oh my god, you're so beautiful." He moved the lace of my bra down, exposing a swollen nipple. "These are the most beautiful breasts." He sucked my nipple and bit down gently. He moved side-to-side, licking and biting my nipples until they were hard and sensitive.

He pulled me up to sitting, pulled the pajama top away and took off the bra. He leaned down and cupped both my breasts in his hands. He pressed them together and rubbed one nipple with his thumb while he bit and sucked on the other. My back arched and I pulled him back down on the bed with me.

INVITATION

He moved between my legs and lowered himself. I was wild with desire. Every part of me ached with the need for him. He continued kissing me and moaning softly in my ear. It made me crazy. I grabbed his ass and pressed up against his hardness, my legs wrapped around him, pinning him in exactly the right position to give pressure and pleasure to just the right place.

He grabbed my hands and pinned them over my head, laughing. He knew I was feeling good. He knew he was the reason. "Keep your hands up here," he ordered. I grasped onto the bars of my bed, but my body continued to move under him. I closed my eyes. I was gone. He could do anything.

He stood up to pull off my pajama bottoms. He ran his hands down the sides of my hips. "Oh, you look so good. I just want to stare at you."

"Don't you dare," I gasped. "Touch me. Please, touch me."

"Where?" he licked my abdomen and ran his fingers lightly up my inner thighs. He stroked the fabric of my underwear, everywhere but my sweetest spot. My head swung back and forth, my mind lost to the gathering waves of pleasure.

"Do you want me to lick you?" he teased. A cry of pleasure escaped my mouth. All I could say was "Please."

"Please what?"

"Please lick me."

The words turned us both on even more.

He moved back on the bed and took hold of my panties. He moved them slowly down my hips. When I lifted my hips to help him, he kissed the top of my mound and pressed down with his mouth. I cried out again.

When my panties were entirely off he suddenly stopped moving. I looked up at him. "I want you to catch your breath," he said, "I'm going to take my time with this."

I tried to calm my body down but it was so far gone. He moved back between my legs and began to kiss my mound. I could tell it was swollen and dripping and hot. I heard him inhaling. "You smell so good." My hands moved to grab his head, but he pushed them away. "Back above your head, now! This is going to be slow and hot. You'll have to beg me to let you come."

He took his two thumbs and ran them softly down the edges of my cleft. He pulled back my outer lips and blew gently on my pussy. I moaned louder. Then he started taking tiny licks all around my inner lips.

"You taste amazing. I'm just going to stay right here licking you like a popsicle." He started low and worked up towards my aching, desperate clitoris.

His tongue darted in and out, driving me wild with increasing pleasure and tension. He put his hands on my lips and spread me wide apart. His tongue circled my tender outer entrance, then pushed its way it. Deeper and deeper he went, his tongue circling and flicking. He stayed in there until I was nearly coming. My hips pressed up hard against him.

He pulled out and breathed softly on me. He was making me wait. He bit my thighs gently while I slowed my breathing.

I tried to relax, but the throbbing in my pussy and around my clitoris was almost unbearable. If he didn't do something, I would have to throw him off the bed and finish things myself. But I really, really wanted him to be the one to make me come. I wanted to come all over his beautiful lips. I wanted his tongue and his fingers buried deep inside me.

He put his mouth over my tiny swollen mound and sucked gently. I cried out, spreading my legs as wide as they would go, pushing my pussy up against his mouth.

I couldn't control myself anymore. I grabbed his head and pulled him into me. As his tongue stroked my clitoris, he put one finger inside me and circled it gently around. Then he did it with two, then three. He increased the pressure on my clitoris, licking me harder in strong circles while he pushed his fingers up deeper inside me. I couldn't distinguish the pleasures anymore. It was all one burning spot of complete ecstasy.

I was beyond words, beyond even moaning. I writhed and bucked against his face, shamelessly pulling his mouth onto me again and again. As the waves crescendoed, every muscle in my legs and ass clenched, desperate for the final lick.

The circles of pleasure started deep within me and exploded out through my center. I screamed out again and again, and kept his face pushed against me as I rode wave after wave of pleasure. "Oh Liam, Oh Liam," I panted. When the spasms finally stopped I lay still as a stone, completely unable to move.

He kissed his way back up my body, wiping his mouth on the sheet before covering my still gasping mouth with his. When my hips had stopped rolling, and I was breathing more smoothly, he whispered in my ear. "And that was just my mouth, baby. Wait 'til you see what I can do with my cock."

When my mind had stopped reeling and I could breathe again, I turned towards Liam and kissed him gently. I trailed my hand down his stomach, through the line of hairs leading to his cock and took hold of it. "Your turn."

He clutched me tight to him, kissing my mouth hard, and cupping a breast in his hands. "I won't last long." I could feel him hot and throbbing. "Do you want me to lick you?" I teased. "Say, please."

"Jesus woman, just talking to you makes me want to come."

"I think we can do better than that." I went down on him and sucked him hard and fast. Within seconds he was exploding in my mouth.

We fell asleep and rested like, well, I was going to say we slept like babies; but in reality we slept like tired young people who had just had really great orgasms.

CHAPTER EIGHTEEN

In the morning we lay wrapped around each other, enjoying the chance to sleep past 6am. Eventually, though, we needed to get up and eat.

Luckily we were at my place, so there was food. My legs were still too wobbly to have walked very far. I made toast and eggs and we sat at the table, enjoying the beams of sunlight that were warming our pale winter skin. I held out my arm and laughed, "I look like a ghost."

"You look gorgeous."

"Stop."

"No. Say it. 'I look gorgeous.'"

"I look gorgeous. For a ghost."

Liam leaped out of his chair and ran towards me. I put my hands over my head, cowering in my chair. He stopped dead in his tracks. His voice was warm with regret and concern. "Oh Madison. I wasn't going to hurt you. I just wanted to hold onto you."

I unfolded myself and tried to smile. "Sorry, sorry. I completely overreacted. My fault."

He kneeled down in front of me, put his hands on my knees and leaned close to my face. "Oh, baby. I just want to kill the people who did this to you."

I shook my head sharply and stood up. "No. We're not talking about this. I don't even want this in the room with us. This is an amazing morning..."

He came up behind me and wrapped his arms around me. "I get it. But are you okay? I'm so sorry if I scared you."

"I'm fine," I snapped. I turned to tuck my head under his chin. He held me even tighter.

"Okay, then. Why don't we get cleaned up and get out of here for a bit."

I stood back a bit to look up at him. "Is that allowed?" He laughed. "No," I persisted, "I mean does that fall within our rules? I'm starting to get confused." And it was true. I was so confused. I was starting to see that it could be hard to simply "have fun" together once a week or so, or at least it was becoming hard for me. We really weren't just having one-night stands of straight up sex. Liam was kind and gentle and generous.

He sat back down and pulled me to him. "I know what you mean. How about this? Let's get dressed. Then we'll take a walk and decide if we're allowed to take walks together."

I laughed and felt instantly better. "Okay, sounds good. But I'm going to have a shower first." I started to walk away, but turned back to him. "I want you to know that, whatever this is, is helping me. I love that you don't treat me like some damaged, fragile thing. I don't want pity, okay? This is working because you treat me like an adult."

"Okay."

I left Liam on the couch. I handed him the remote control, and the TV sprang to life. I figured he'd be amused for an hour or two.

In the bathroom, I stopped to brush my teeth again. Eggs are great for my energy level, but not so great for my breath. I stared at my face, trying to see what Liam said he saw. It was impossible to believe. I started to doubt him again. "Oh, enough," I thought to myself. "Stupid brain. You have the weekend off. Body, you're in charge." I pushed my shoulders high, trying for confidence or at least a good stab at faking it.

God I love showers. They are an under-appreciated miracle of the modern world. Warm water hits my face and I am a different person. I felt my muscles getting soft and warm. I washed my hair first, then soaped up my body. I was just rinsing off when I felt the cool air of the door being opened. "Liam?" The door closed and his shadow appeared on the other side of the shower curtain. I knew what he meant, what he wanted, but I wanted to stall for a minute. I needed time to process this.

"Okay," I squeaked with fake cheerfulness, "I'm almost done! Just give me another minute!" Or two, or three or ten.

"I want to come in with you." It was more of a command than a request. "I want to look at you."

"You've seen me."

"In the dark. It's time. Can I come in?" He waited a moment and I didn't answer. "I'm coming in."

I turned toward the jet so my back was to him. He came up behind me and stroked my hair and shoulders. As soon as he touched me, the fear was gone. Inhibitions seemed childish. Every action showed care and desire.

He pushed my wet hair over my shoulder and began kissing all down my back. He licked at the water trickling down. I shivered with pleasure. He reached around me to lift the soap from the rack and began massaging my shoulders with the suds. He moved down my back, my ass, and my legs. He stood up and started again with my shoulders. The soap helped him slide effortlessly down to my breasts. Rubbing, circling, stroking. He pinched my nipples and the shock of it travelled down into my abdomen and pussy.

I was already warm and swollen, and I started throbbing almost instantly. I tried to turn around to kiss him, but he stopped me.

"Don't turn around. It's too much to see you all at once. I need to pace myself. I'm going to focus on the back of you for a minute." He tickled the skin in the small of my back. He rubbed my ass, then grabbed my waist to pull me into him. I leaned back and felt his erection pressing against my back. His hardness, his excitement both turned me on and made me braver. What wonderful proof that I was attractive and appealing to him.

INVITATION

I reached my arms up behind me to grasp the sides of his head. I arched my back and pushed my breasts forward. He massaged them faster and harder, rubbing his thumb roughly over my tingling nipples. His left arm stayed wrapped around me, just under my ribcage, but his right hand moved lower and lower.

My body had no fight in it. I wanted that hand on my throbbing mound. His middle finger moved lightly down the center of my cleft.

"Oh, you're so slippery. You're so ready." His finger pressed harder and moved rhythmically up and down as I gasped and moaned. I could hardly stand. He cupped his hand all around my throbbing sweet spot then and started with wide circles, round and round, coming closer and closer to my aching clitoris. I leaned back against him, and put my hands behind us, grabbing his ass, trying to remain standing.

He was holding me with one arm, and the right hand, cupped around my center was pressing upward with intensity and rhythm. He was nearly lifting me off the ground. I twisted my face towards him. I needed desperately to feel his mouth. My breasts, my mouth, my pussy all ached for him. He rubbed faster and faster and I cried out, pushing hard against his hand. "I'm coming," I choked. "Don't stop. Harder. Rub me harder...." My entire body clenched for a moment, then exploded in exquisite spasms.

Liam waited for my body to calm, then turned off the water. He helped me to turn toward him and said, "Let me taste you." He spread my legs apart, and then the folds of my pussy and took a long slow lick from top to bottom. I shuddered with pleasure.

CHAPTER NINETEEN

"You. Bed." Liam looked at me. The gentle, tender Liam was still in there somewhere, but I was seeing a new, fiercer, face. He kissed me hard, opening my mouth wide, moving his tongue deep inside me. I was being devoured. "I am going to have you right now."

He stepped out of the tub and wrapped himself in a towel. Then he wrapped me in a towel and lifted me over the edge of the tub. He carried me straight to the bed. He placed me down gently, but then ripped my towel open to stare at me. He quickly looked away. "Jesus, it's like starting into the sun." He looked up at my face. "You're perfect," he growled and kissed me. He pressed down hard on my lips.

"I have to have you," he was looking into my eyes. He didn't want to stop, I wasn't sure if he even could. But I was ready.

"Okay," I said.

"And next time we'll take it slow. But..." He had put his finger back in my cleft and was moving it up and down again, "Oh, oh god. But I need you now."

I felt the same way. The sensations on my lips and my clitoris were fantastic, but there was a throbbing ache deep inside me that only one thing could touch.

He climbed on top of me and kissed me hard once more, then began his rapid decent. He stopped briefly to tongue my nipples until I was crying out and pushing his head down towards where I needed him most. He pushed my legs apart, wide, and began moving his fingers around my pussy, caressing the lips and the tender flesh at the entrance to my core. He moved a finger gently in and out, and started to suck and lick my clitoris. I shuddered and grabbed his head, pressing him into my pussy.

I had to come soon. I had to come or I would go insane. The throbbing deep inside had to be taken care of.

I grabbed his hair and pulled him back up toward my face. I bent my knees, trapping him in my valley. I felt his cock, hard along my cleft. I tried to maneuver my hips to get it inside me, but with one hand he pinned my hips down and started teasing me with the tip of his cock: tiny movements at my entrance in and out. My tunnel was so swollen it felt almost like pain. My eyes clenched shut. Nothing else existed except that area where we were connecting. I didn't feel anything except that building excruciating pleasure.

"Oh, fuck me," I begged, but still he just teased. My legs wrapped around his ass and pulled him straight down, into me, into my slick, smooth, swollen tunnel. We both made a deep primal sound. The most basic and wonderful of pleasures was being met.

He started to move slowly, and I could feel his firm width and length pushing at the sides of me. I could feel his head reaching deeply, pushing itself into my willing, wet, flesh. I was full of him. The size of him pushed on every fold of me. The pressure was intense and extraordinary.

He started to pull out again, but my body wanted him right where he was. My core spasmed, circling him in its embrace. He cried out in pleasure and surprise. He, like me, was beyond control. He pulled far back then, almost out, and drove into me hard, pushing up until I cried out.

He did it again and again, rubbing my walls with his head and his thickness, slamming himself against me. He shifted his position slightly so that his shaft rubbed my clitoris as he rode me, and I was soon wild, an animal, scratching at his back and his ass, screaming for him to fuck me and fuck me.

I came hard, screaming out "Liam!" while I grabbed his ass and push myself up against him again and again, prolonging the beautiful waves that rushed through me. Finally, he was coming too. His eyes were clenched shut, his teeth gritted. The pounding grew even stronger as he cried out and slammed into me, pushing me up towards the headboard. I spread my legs wider and wider, wanting to welcome him deeper and deeper inside of me.

Soon his ass was clenching hard and he was calling out, "Oh god, oh my god." His hand was under me, grabbing my ass, holding it still and in position as he rammed himself up into me. He let out a final, deep groan.

His body softened slowly as he lay down on top of me. He held his weight off my chest with his strong arms, and kissed the side of my face and neck slowly and softly. I traced my fingers along his spine. We stayed that way, loving each other's bodies, calming them down.

After a long happy time, he tried to roll over; but I wrapped my legs around his and pinned him in place. I liked feeling his cock still just inside of me. I liked the weight of him pushing me down, tethering me to the world. I could pretend I was safe and maybe even loved.

CHAPTER TWENTY

The walk was forgotten. We spent most of that day in bed. In the evening, Liam left my bed reluctantly and started gathering his things.

"I'm on call tomorrow," he said, "or I'd stay all night. I hate being on call on Sundays. It makes the week seem twice as long."

"It's okay. If you stay much longer, I think my heart will just give out." I followed him out of bed and put on my robe. "Can I feed you at least?" He opened my robe and scraped his teeth across a nipple. The pleasure was intense and immediate, but I pushed him away laughing.

"Be gone with you. I'm going to be in the library tomorrow afternoon..." I wanted to say, come and find me. Was that was a boyfriend/girlfriend thing? I didn't want to lose what I had with Liam, so I stopped myself. I couldn't appear too demanding or clingy. That was a turn-off. Right? I was getting a headache worrying about what I could and could not do.

"You have cute little worry lines between your eyebrows. Getting a headache?"

"Sort of."

"What's a sort of headache?" He moved toward me and started softly kneading the muscles of my upper back. He had a magic touch, but a headache wasn't really the problem.

"I need some guidelines."

He sank into my couch and patted the seat beside him. "God, you sound like a medical intern now!"

"Not medical guidelines. 'Us' guidelines. Like right there. Am I allowed to say 'us' guidelines, or is that being presumptuous or controlling?"

He rubbed his head. "Your tension is contagious." Then he looked at me and smiled. "I thought we were keeping this simple."

"Me, too." He leaned back from me, resting his weight on the arm of the sofa. In all honesty I think I was actually relieved. I didn't want to be the one demanding emotional distance. That made me feel like I was damaged or incomplete somehow; it seemed better for him to say it, and then for me to be secretly relieved.

I had sworn to myself I wouldn't get distracted from school, and here I was spending all day in bed, and I was probably going to be up half the night worrying about things. "But then we were going to go for a walk, which sounds like dating sort of stuff."

"Which we're not." I was taken aback a little by how quickly he put that out there. "Look, get your work schedule." He got his phone from the table. I got up to get my phone and scrolled through to find the days I was working, and the nights I'd be at the hospital.

"Okay, so, these are the weekend days and evenings we both have off." It was a depressingly small number. "So, the first question is, 'Are you seeing other people?'"

I sort of snorted at that. "I think you'd know the answer to that. A month ago I was pretty much terrified of men, so, I think I'll limit myself to one for now." I wasn't sure I wanted the answer to what came next, but I had to ask, "Are you?"

He looked down at his hands in his lap and rocked back and forth a little. Even though I supposedly didn't care about him at all, I could barely breathe waiting for his reply. Finally he shook his head, looked up and said, "No. No, I'm not." There was a brief uncomfortable moment, after which he asked, "So, should we pencil each other in for the next two weeks?"

I laughed at loud, but he wasn't kidding. He was right. If we didn't actively plan, our only meetings would be over red Jell-O in the cafeteria. "How often do you want to?"

"Woman, if it's up to me I'll be seeing you completely naked at every available opportunity." He pulled me closer.

"Okay."

He moved back and looked at me. "You don't seem too convinced."

I couldn't even put it into words for myself yet, so I had no chance of explaining it to Liam. But, especially with Chloe gone and having to spend every spare minute at the hospital or the library, I never seemed to see any of my friends.

I was lonely, I think. It was that simple. And the idea of going to a movie or to dinner, hell the idea of getting to know something about him besides his prowess in bed was becoming really appealing. I don't think I was in love already by then, but I really, REALLY liked him. I liked him enough to know I couldn't blow it with some big emotional ambush.

"No, of course I'm convinced."

"But..."

"Well, if we happen to be hungry, or there happens to be a great movie on..." I started.

"Or our legs cramp up from Kama Sutra positions and we need to walk it out?"

I smacked him, but laughed. "Yes, exactly!"

"Come here," he took my hand and pulled me towards him. "I don't know how to play this either. The thing is, I'm probably leaving in a couple months, so it's going to work itself out anyway."

I didn't move but a lump formed in my throat. "Why? Where are you going?"

He kissed the top of my head. "I've been trying to get a rotation in LA. I probably won't get chosen, but I'm doing Emergency Med and it would be a great experience."

I hadn't even known what his specialty was. I thought he was in Cardiology! Why was I pretending this was more than it was? I really didn't know much about him or his life at all. He continued on, "So, I'm sure you can tell I'm really into you. But I can't get too deep into something, you know?"

I nodded my head. I DID know. Who knew where I would be a year from now, or two or three? I could end up in a completely different city, too. Starting any sort of relationship was crazy. But it still hurt to hear him sounding like another commitment-phobic jerk. I knew I wasn't being fair, but tough. It was damn confusing.

He sat up straighter. "So, I guess I'm going to sound like a real asshole, but I think we need to either decide we can both handle this staying a physical thing, or we should just try to stay away from each other. I think I could really fall for you, and I can't let that happen."

I sat quietly for a minute.

"You think I'm an asshole," he said sadly. But I shook my head.

"I think we're both assholes. But we've worked so hard to get here. Our lives come second to work. That's just the way it is. Even if we were both in the same place... I mean, seriously, checking our phones for possible dates two weeks from now? You're right. It's impossible."

"So, which is it going to be? Are you in or out? I totally get if you need to just cool it and not have to deal with all this..."

As he talked I got up and stood in front of him. He was dressed, but I had just my flimsy robe on. I looked right into his sparkling blue eyes. "I have a feeling this is sort of a once-in-lifetime thing. And I'll take it as long as I can get it."

I reached to his waist, and pulled his t-shirt over his head. I unbuttoned and unzipped his pants. He hadn't put socks on yet, so once I had pushed his pants and underwear down to the floor and kicked them to the side, he was completely naked.

"Once again there is not enough time for me to really have my way with you..." He smiled up at me and leaned back. He reached his hands out.

INVITATION

"Just a minute." I kneeled between his legs and stroked his cock softly. I licked it like an ice cream until he was hard as a rock and pulling my hair. Then I stood up and let the robe slide off me. He stared at every part of me. I watched his cock throb and bounce. He started to touch himself, but I said, "No, no. That's mine."

"Let me touch you." He tried to grab between my legs.

"There's no need. I'm already dripping wet."

He put his hands to his face and leaned back. "This isn't playing fair."

I moved back towards him. I straddled him, but didn't sink down onto him. I grabbed him and put him at my entrance. He felt it wet and hot and pulled me down onto him, burying himself inside me. He grabbed my hips and moved me up and down. God he was strong. I started rocking my hips in rhythm. We fit together so perfectly. It just felt so easy and right.

I grabbed his shoulders and leaned back. He bit my nipples. I squeezed my core tight around him. He grabbed my ass hard and started ramming up into me.

"Touch yourself now," he ordered. I put my fingers into my cleft and felt his cock moving in and out beneath them. "Touch yourself. I want to watch." He slowed his thrusts and leaned back, looking down to where my fingers where.

He lifted my hand to his mouth and sucked on my fingers. Then he put my hand down on my sensitive place and started moving it in circles. At the same time he started gently, slowly thrusting up into me again. He clutched my ass and moved in rhythm with my building tension. I circled my clit harder and faster. He watched.

"That is so sexy," he panted.

I was beyond speech. His pounding became harder and faster. I rubbed my clit until I cried out incoherently. He slammed into me once more, driving up all the way into me, and then he too tumbled over the edge. He crushed me against his chest and buried his face in my hair. "Oh, baby," he chanted until his breath slowed.

Eventually, we pulled ourselves apart and got dressed.

"I really have to go now."

"I know."

This time he was the one with little frown lines on his fore-head. I rubbed them away and smiled. "Penny for your thoughts?"

But he didn't smile back. He just wrapped his arms around me, kissed me on the forehead, and said, "I think we're in trouble."

And then he left.

CHAPTER TWENTY-ONE

The next day was a study day for me. I had a midway exam coming up and wanted to get a great mark. Anything I could do to get Dr. Olsen to like me without slime ball's help was a good thing.

I was exhausted, but in a nice way. Being tired because I'd been busy the day before with someone amazing was entirely different from being wiped-out from too many days and nights on call. A shower woke me up a bit and loosened my sore muscles.

I grabbed my laptop, some books and a few protein bars and headed for the library. The rain continued on. I usually study at the bigger Humanities library on campus, but the hospital was much closer, and I was already frozen, so I made my way there.

I found the study area deserted, which was great. I grabbed the carrel in the farthest, quietest corner and got to work. I mainly had a lot of memorizing to do: bizarre symptoms, drug dosages, stuff like that. None of it was too hard by itself; it was just the amount of stuff to remember that got overwhelming at times. I could see how all the residents had developed their severe caffeine addictions.

I worked for about three hours and then needed to stretch my legs. I was chilled, of course, so I headed for the cafeteria to get some tea. I guess I was secretly hoping to see Liam. I figured even catching a glimpse would help me pass the rest of the day.

But there was no sign of him. He was probably swamped down in Emergency. Usually I would try to do something nice, like take him something to eat, but I wasn't his girlfriend.

The more I thought about it, the more I realized I was playing a pretty dangerous game. Seeing him would only make me think about him more. I needed to get better at dividing my school and work life with my extracurricular activities. This might be one of those reasons to not date a coworker. Not that we were dating. Or whatever.

So, instead of tracking him down or paging him, I went back to the study room and did my best to play the dutiful student. By 3:30, I had been at it for seven hours and my brain needed a time out. I decided I'd go home.

When I finally left the hospital, I found that the rain had stopped. It wasn't exactly nice weather, but it meant I didn't have to lift my hood, hunch over, and run home as fast as I could. In fact, I wanted to get a little fresh air. So, I walked back to my new favorite lingerie shop. Meredith, the classy salesperson was there again and quickly gathered up all her favorites for me to try on.

I expected to feel as excited and pretty as I had last time. Right in the middle of putting the pale pink teddy on, though, I realized that I didn't need any lingerie. Liam was leaving in a couple of weeks. I didn't know how long he was going for, but from the way he talked about it, it was clear that he thought we were only going to be getting together until he left.

I don't know why I was so shocked by my feelings, but I really was. I was going to miss him. I was going to miss him so much. My heart sank in my chest and I dropped onto the bench in the change room. I felt hollowed out and empty. Whatever limitations we had put on our relationship, it had brought me a sense of peace and happiness that had been missing from my life for a long time. Thinking of life after he'd gone was unbearable.

I started crying, and when the salesperson, Meredith, came to the back, I tried to pull myself together. It didn't work, though, and I ended up just making up some silly excuse and burning it out of the store. I speed-walked home sniffling all the way.

When I got home, I cranked up the heat, stripped down and ran a bath. I tried to relax into the warm water, but the warmth and comfort of it made me miss Liam. It was time to admit it. I was in deep. I liked him. A LOT. And I was pretty sure he liked me.

I got out of the bath, put on my robe, and then sat on my bed staring at my phone. Should I call him? Should I text him something flirty and casual? Should I just be a grown up and say I wanted to talk to him? And then be brave, and go for it, and tell him I wanted whatever "it" was to be something more?

Right when I had convinced myself to "woman up" and call Liam, I received the following text from him:

Madison, you're so great. But I can't do this. Sorry.

And my heart slammed shut once more.

CHAPTER TWENTY-TWO

He was gone.

His rotation in Cardiology at my hospital was finished. He had moved on to something else in the hospital on the other side of the city.

He didn't call. Or text. Or email. He disappeared. His body was gone, but the hole he'd left inside me had weight and power. I felt heavy and sick, and miserably lonely.

The days ran together. The nights were worse. I began looking forward to being on call, and took on extra shifts. It won me some brownie points, but the real goal for me was oblivion. I was too busy to think and too tired to feel.

Late one night, though, after twelve days had passed (but who was counting?) I sent him a text. Just a stupid short, "Hi, how are you? How's the new rotation?" bullshit sort of message where you try to sound really casual, but you end up crying yourself to sleep about it because they don't answer back.

I was glad that this had happened while I was on my Pediatrics rotation. No other ward could have cheered me up, at least a little. The kids were happy to see me. Lots of the parents were exhausted and strung out on fear, but they seemed to calm down around me, so the nurses started calling me when things were spiraling out of control.

I surprised myself. I had been such an isolated loner, but it turns out that I liked talking to patients and their families. Helping them understand things and feel better made me feel useful. And it kept me busy.

INVITATION

Little Alex had healed up enough to go home, and now I was only seeing him from time to time at one of the outpatient clinics. I thought all my patients were brave and wonderful little people, but Alex and I had struck up some kind of bond. I had been collecting cars and monster trucks for him whenever I saw one, and he loved to bring the whole collection in to show the nurses and me. He had a face that just made you feel better. All long eyelashes and summery freckles.

One afternoon, after I'd finished checking his vitals and reviewing his blood work with his parents, I got paged to see Dr. Olsen. I had really been working hard and, I thought, keeping myself out of trouble, so I was surprised to be summoned to her office. I didn't know why she would need to see me.

Here I can only say that it is important to not forget about the snakes and rats of this world. Because, where an actual human being might notice you're a little down and give you a break, these life forms prefer to move in for the kill.

I made my way as quickly as I could to her office. It was on another floor at the far end of the hospital. Even after practically running, and skipping the slow-moving elevators to take the stairs, it took a few minutes to get there. She was checking the time on her phone when I knocked on her door. She looked up at me, already annoyed.

"Sorry, Dr. Olsen. I was over at the Outpatient Clinic…"

She waved her hand at me. "Never mind, Madison. Have a seat."

This is when I noticed Owen was already in the office. He was sitting in a chair next to the one I was supposed to take. I pulled my chair closer to me, away from him and sat down. He looked annoyed, but then again, when didn't he?

The office was small and cluttered, which surprised me. Dr. Olsen seemed like a person who would have furniture made of sterilized glass. But instead, she had warm wood furniture and pale yellow walls. What you could see on the walls, anyway, because they were crowded with drawings made for her by hundreds of little kids. I looked around at all the bursts of color and made the mistake of relaxing just a little.

"Dr. Humphries has brought some concerns to my attention," she started.

I looked over at Owen who refused to make eye contact with me. I was completely confused. "I'm sorry?" I started. "I don't understand."

She folded her hands together and leaned back in her chair. "I can't be everywhere at once, obviously." I nodded. "So, I rely on the senior residents to keep me informed about people's progress." I nodded again, but my stomach was sinking. Where could this be going?

"He tells me you did poorly on the first exam."

I started to disagree, but she put her hand up. "Please don't interrupt me."

I sat back in my chair to listen. "He also tells me that you've been carrying on with one of the other residents and that this seems to have impacted your work."

She leaned forward, waiting for a response from me. Other people would probably come up with great arguments on the spot, but I was just frightened, and completely flustered. Whose business was it who I saw outside the hospital? And why would they say I hadn't been working hard? I put in more hours than any other student. And what was she talking about with the exam? I got 80% on it. Not amazing, obviously, but cause enough to be dragged into a meeting? What was going on?

"Dr. Olsen, I apologize. This is a surprise to me." I swallowed hard, forcing my voice not to crack. "I think the rotation has gone well. I'm learning so much . . ."

She threw her hands up again, signaling me to stop talking. "Be that as it may, Owen, Dr. Humphries, has very kindly offered to give you some additional assistance. So I suggest you take him up on it." She turned to look at him. "Perhaps you could speak with Madison this afternoon after final rounds and make some plans?"

He nodded, pretending to be the overworked but keen resident, happy to help out the green youngster.

"Great." Dr. Olsen stood, gathered some charts and herded us out of the room. "You have two weeks left until the final evaluation."

I walked away from Owen before he could even open his slimy mouth. The lying, manipulative pig!

I actually walked to the entrance of the hospital and stood there considering whether I should just leave. I wasn't sure I could face it. The other men had used drugs and a camera to nearly destroy me, and now this creep was going to use his authority to bring me to heel.

I walked outside to try to breathe. I sat on a bench, the same bench I had waited for Liam on. I remembered everything wonderful about him, and I briefly felt warmer and a little better. Before I could stop myself, I texted him, "I need help with Owen. Please write back." I waited for ten minutes, trying not to stare at the phone.

Eventually, an icy blast of freezing wet rain slapped me in the face and brought me back to reality. Liam was an asshole, just like all the rest of them. And at that moment, I hated him most of all.

CHAPTER TWENTY-THREE

Because I wanted the afternoon to drag on forever, it flew by. Before I could really make any sort of survival plan, rounds were over and it was time to meet up with Owen.

He was waiting by the locker rooms.

"I thought maybe we'd eat." It was an order, not a question.

I had my coat halfway on, so I started removing it. I thought we were going to the cafeteria and I was relieved. What could he do with a bunch of witnesses around?

But that wasn't the plan. "Not in this dump. I want some real food. Let's go." He held his arm out, leading the way to the parkade.

"I can't go far," I told him. "As you know, I need to do a lot of extra studying, so I can't afford to waste time on dinner." I tried to keep the venom out of my voice, but I don't think I was too successful.

"Tonight you're studying with me, so you can spare the time." He put his hand against the small of my back and pushed me along. I sidestepped to get away from him. "We could head to my place if you want," he offered.

"No. Someplace public will be fine. Let's skip food and just go to the library." I almost added, "To get this over with", but fortunately my internal sensors were working at least a little.

"Nope, we're eating."

That was that. We walked to the parkade and got in his car. I suppose I was supposed to ooh and ahh over it, but seriously guys, enough with the cars. Ditch the fancy wheels and get a decent personality instead.

We went to a restaurant I had never heard of. I was underdressed and uncomfortable. He ordered wine and tried to flirt.

I asked him question after question about medicine. At first he enjoyed the attention and the chance to show off. But as he tried to turn the conversation to more personal matters and I continued with my evasive medical quiz, he became increasingly annoyed. The wine he was drinking didn't help.

He worked his way through three courses while I played with a cup of soup. There was a lump in my throat, and my stomach churned with acid.

"Let's share a dessert." He was trying to prolong the evening. "Girls like chocolate, right?" He didn't wait for my response. The waitress came over and he said, "We'll have the mousse. Two spoons."

"One spoon," I countered. "I don't like chocolate." Which is actually true, but even if chocolate was my nirvana I wouldn't have touched that dessert.

I looked up at the waitress, "And maybe you could call me a cab when you have a second?"

"I'm taking you home," he commanded.

"You're not taking anybody home," I said. "You've had a bottle and a half of wine."

His face got red and his hands clenched the tablecloth. "I'm driving us . . ."

Before he could finish, the waitress interrupted. "We're not allowed to let anyone drive if they're intoxicated. It's the law." She touched me on the shoulder. "So, I'll just call for two cabs, then." We made eye contact and I felt a brief warm flash of sisterly solidarity. Then she left to make the calls and get the mousse.

The dessert was eaten and the bill taken care of. I let Owen pay for my soup. I left the waitress a big tip.

We got our coats and waited outside on the sidewalk for the cabs. We didn't speak. I was relieved. Owen said only, "Bitch," and I didn't know if he meant the waitress or me. It didn't matter, really. I knew I'd be the one to pay for it. I knew there was going to be a huge price to pay for my insubordination. But at that moment, when the cab pulled up and I got in, alone, what I felt was the pure pleasure of safety and escape.

CHAPTER TWENTY-FOUR

That night I dreamed of Liam: We are on a beach, reclining in long, elegant deck chairs. The chairs have long armrests and thick, comfortable cushions. Our bodies feel warm and loose and sexy. The sun is perfect, heating our most sensual areas. Gentle breezes make our skin tingle. I feel the warm pleasure of it on my skin.

Our arms stretch between the chairs and we hold hands. In the dream I am drifting off to sleep, but Liam stands and moves to my chair. He starts to smooth oil onto me, first along my arms, concentrating on that tender skin along the inside. He tucks a hand into each cup of my orange bikini and massages my breasts until the nipples are hard. He pushes the fabric down until he can take each nipple in his mouth. He licks and sucks on them. He scrapes them gently with his teeth. He bites just hard enough to make me moan.

I want to open my eyes. I want to grab him and kiss him. But in the dream the heat from the sun, and the pleasure from Liam paralyze me. My body aches and throbs. The wait for him to find my most sensitive place is unbearable.

His lips are suddenly on mine, and they are on fire. It is not a kiss; it is a communion with this beautiful man. We are connected and the electricity flows through us.

He places his hand on the side of my face and pulls me closer, harder into his kiss. He is kneeling beside my chair and running his hands along my body as though I am an exquisite sculpture.

Christina Hoffman

The top of my tiny bikini is fastened in the front, and Liam undoes it slowly. Now my breasts are exposed to the wind and the sun. The arousal is escalating. My eyes are still closed, my body still and accepting. I feel no self-consciousness, no inhibitions.

Liam places his palm flat on my stomach and gently begins tracing tiny circles. The circles increase in size, and he is soon brushing against the edge of my bikini bottoms. My hips rise up to meet his hand, but he gently pushes them down. This will be slow. He is taking his time.

He goes to the bottom of the chaise, near my feet. He holds each ankle, and gently spreads my legs apart, exposing my inner legs. He begins to rub oil along my legs, swirling his fingers up higher and higher, until they are almost at the fabric of my bathing suit. My eyes remain closed. He pauses, and my body waits for the next touch; lips, nipples, clit, all swelling to meet his fingers, aching for his touch.

His mouth returns to mine, and there is a hunger and an urgency to our kissing now. He sticks his fingers into my mouth and groans into my neck as I suck them. He takes his wet fingers and circles around the fabric of my bikini bottoms until I am writhing and begging to be touched. Then he slips his hand down the front of my bathing suit, sliding his wet finger into my already swollen, hot cleft. I gasp with pleasure. His groan is deep, guttural, the sound of a man trying to stay in control.

He presses down with his whole hand, moving in small circles. The pressure is dispersed, creating new sensations as each part of my center is touched at the same time. My body can't remain still any longer. My back is arching, my hips rocking, pressing myself up into him. My hands clutch at the wooden arms of the chaise, and my head swings slowly back and forth. My lips part and I lick them. I move my hands to my breasts and grab them. Hard. I am so close I am crying for release.

But he stops. I open my eyes then and look up at my beautiful man. In my dream he is mine. And his being mine feels even more amazing than what is happening to my body. The miraculous things happening on my skin and lips and nipples and pussy, pale in comparison to the pleasure and joy and peace that I feel in my heart.

I reach out to pull him to me. I want to feel him pressed all along my body. I want the pressure and pleasure of his long hard cock pressing against the flimsy fabric of my bathing suit. I want him to rip it off and slam himself into me deeper and deeper. I want to wrap my whole body around him and keep him there forever.

But he shakes his head and smiles at me when I try to pull him down. He pushes me back gently, so I am reclining against the tilt of the chair. He moves behind the chair and changes the position so that I am nearly flat.

Then he moves to the bottom of the chair and takes my left ankle in his hands. He runs his fingers more roughly this time up my inner thigh, almost scratching them. He massages the highest part of my thigh roughly, so that the movement also moves my clitoris slightly. I am quickly back to the almost unbearable need for release. Then he takes my leg, bends it at the knee, and drapes it over the long wooden arm of the chair. The wood is old and warm and smooth.

My leg is lifted up and my center is more exposed than ever. Liam does the same with my right leg, until I am reclined, with my legs lifted and spread. I am completely open and vulnerable and desperate for his touch.

He sits astride the chair facing me and begins to rub both hands down my inner thighs, coming closer to my pussy each time. Finally he takes his thumbs and runs them down my cleft, just grazing my sweetest spot, and igniting pleasure everywhere he touches. He pushes his thumbs up into my entrance, and the ache for him becomes all-encompassing. Nothing but his hands exists.

He unties the strings of my bikini bottom, and pulls the little scrap of orange fabric down. I am lost. Beyond thought. I am no longer on earth.

He parts me with his left hand and strokes each delicate lip with his right. He slides his fingers into me, slowly, tauntingly, and moves them in wide circles, to touch each special spot. My eyes are closed, so I don't see his mouth moving towards my swollen sensitive bud, but I feel his warm breath on me and I know what's about to happen.

As his fingers push and rub and circle, his tongue takes tiny licks of my pussy. Every muscle in my body trembles with desire, anticipating when he will land on my clitoris. My hands claw at my inner thighs, pulling them even farther apart, and my hips rise up, desperately trying to steer him to the perfect place.

He comes right up against my sweet spot, but refuses to lick it. He teases and teases, until I am beyond myself. I am grabbing his head, my hands entwined in that beautiful thick hair, and I am pulling him onto me, slamming up against his tongue and his teeth. He is laughing deeply, a man pleased with himself, enjoying his work. I hold him exactly where I need him. Every muscle is taut. Sweat drips down my back, my thighs.

He takes my bud in his mouth and flicks it with his tongue until I am gasping and writhing and sobbing. He places his whole mouth on me and starts to suck. I am begging him not to stop. I have no shame. I am screaming out, and slamming myself against his lips. The circles of pleasure build until they are almost excruciating, so much pressure contained in one tiny spot...

And then they explode outward, rocking my body with spasm after spasm of complete ecstasy and release. They move through me over and over, like waves in the ocean. I ride them and ride them. I can barely breathe and I'm still whimpering. Liam pushes his hand against my pussy and I ride his hand, too. The waves go on and on.

In my dream I want Liam more than I ever have. My body is filled with ecstasy and electricity, but there is still that one deep place begging for attention and relief. I raise my arms to grab hold of him and pull him in, but when I open my eyes . . . he is gone.

INVITATION

I woke up in my bed, surrounded by the ghost of Liam. The room was cold and silent. I had never felt more alone.

CHAPTER TWENTY-FIVE

In the morning I woke up slowly, clinging to the dream. The dream wasn't just a visual memory. I still felt him. I smelled the suntan lotion on him. I remembered feeling that I loved him. Every part of me, every sense, remembered Liam.

I clung to that feeling as long as I could, but eventually it faded and I was awake. I felt the loss all over again. Before the dream, some of the pain of losing Liam had faded a little. But it was back with a vengeance. My body felt like it was filled with a dark, heavy misery. My muscles and bones ached. It was like the flu, without the fever. Instead I couldn't stop shivering.

It was the first Saturday I'd had off in a long time. I got up and made tea. I splashed water on my face and tried to wake up enough to get some studying done.

My body could still feel Liam's touch. I could see him and smell him. But the worst was the ache inside of missing him. In the dream I was happy. I felt safe and cared for.

I tried to resist it, I really did. I knew that if I could keep myself awake, go for a walk, fill my brain with medical facts, the dream would dissipate and I would be free of its painful hold on me.

But I missed him so much. The dream, the feelings were so real. I knew I was torturing myself. I knew it was healthier to block it out. But I wasn't strong enough. I crawled back into bed, and wrapped myself in my warmest blanket. I closed my eyes and drifted back into the world of Liam. I was like an addict needing one more taste.

INVITATION

I didn't wake up again until the evening. The loneliness was deeper than ever. How could I have cared so much for him? How could I have misread the signs? I had been as cold and suspicious as I knew how to be, and I still thought we were both feeling the same things. How did he do those things with me, and say those wonderful things and then just turn it all off? How could it mean nothing to him? How could I mean nothing?

I was on call again Sunday morning, so I set my alarm. I brushed my teeth and washed my face. And then I went back to bed and slept twelve hours straight.

The next couple of days went by in a blur. I started work Sunday morning at 8am and worked straight through until Monday afternoon at 4pm. There had only been a couple of us on, so we were busy with admissions and emergencies on the ward the whole time. I hadn't screwed up anything major and, best of all, neither Dr. Olsen or Owen had been around.

It was busy, but good. I saw a couple of interesting things in Emergency and got to talk to some great kids. I brought in muffins for the nurses on the ward and practically got a standing ovation. So I went to get coffees for everyone, and then I did get that standing ovation. Working on the weekend can really stink, but the hospital can be a different, friendlier place when the pace slows down and some of the egos are away.

By the end of Monday afternoon, though, I was ready to stumble home, eat some noodles from a Styrofoam cup and head to bed.

I hadn't heard anything from Liam; but I hadn't heard anything from Owen, either. I was beginning to think that I might have been imagining the sinister tone of my encounters with him. Maybe the evening at dinner hadn't been so bad?

You know how it is, though. As soon as I let myself think I might be safe, my damn pager went off. I knew, even before anyone answered who would be calling. Sure enough, it was Owen.

"Time for lesson number two." He announced.

"Owen. Thank you for thinking of me." I was determined to be polite, but firm. "But I've been working thirty-two hours straight and I can hardly remember my name. I cannot study tonight."

"Your name is Madison. The Madison who will fail this rotation if she doesn't meet me in the hallway by my call room in five minutes." He hung up. I slumped down in defeat.

"Bad news?" Cara the charge nurse asked.

"I have to go get 'tutored'," I put the word in brackets.

"You poor kids. Up all night, and now you've got to go to a class, too?" She put her arm on my back and gave it a little rub. The kindness almost brought tears to my eyes. Sometimes I think that this is what people who have a mother get to experience all the time. But I know better than that, really. Plenty of people who have mothers don't get comforting pats on the back. So I pulled myself back from the brink of self-pity and just enjoyed the moment for what it was.

"No," I answered with a sigh. "It's sort of a private class with Dr. Humphries. Dr. Olsen's orders."

She looked up sharply, and I thought she looked alarmed. "That seems weird."

I gave a short, cold laugh. "You have no idea." I put away the charts I was looking at and closed down the screen on the computer. "Wish me luck," I said quietly and wandered away.

CHAPTER TWENTY-SIX

I'm ashamed to say that I didn't put up any fight at all. I just went. I was so tired that everything looked sort of blurry and surreal. I told myself I would just go and pretend to listen and nod at whatever moronic thing the guy was supposedly trying to teach me. I figured just letting him blab on would be faster than arguing about it. Plus we both knew who would win anyway. I decided to conserve what little energy I had and get it over with.

I wanted to change out of my scrubs and lab coat, but thought it would seem like more of a date if I did. So I kept those grubby things on, hoping to repel him with my wrinkled, sleep-deprived looks.

He was leaning against the wall waiting for me. I remember thinking that it was such a shame he was a creep, because he was a nice-looking guy, with shiny blond hair, and a swimmer's shoulders. He had a face that would have been handsome if there had ever been a genuine smile on it.

He looked up at me. "Thought I might hear from you this weekend," he said.

"Was I supposed to call you?" I stopped a few feet away from him. I felt light-headed and put my hand on the wall to keep from falling over.

He shrugged. "Well, if it was my neck on the line, I might show some initiative."

I opened my mouth to mention being on call and how busy we had been, but I stopped myself. It didn't matter. We weren't actually discussing reality.

"Guess you spent your time with Mason instead."

Dr. Mason. Liam. God, I missed him. God, I hated him.

I didn't bother answering Owen. It was none of his damn business, and I sure as hell wasn't going to tell this jerk that I'd been dumped. He'd probably start in with the whole, "I'm a good listener", bullshit again and, in my nearly delirious state I would probably role my eyes and tell him to go to hell.

"So what's so special about him?" Owen demanded. "Everybody's falling all over that guy, all the time. What is it?"

I knew better than to answer. Was it true? Was he trying to hurt me, or stir up trouble? I didn't understand exactly what was happening, but I knew we were into some kind of messed up psychological crap here. Jesus, if only I could have done my Psych rotation first, I might have had some weapons to use on this guy.

My stomach flipped and bile came into my mouth. The exhaustion was winning and my legs grew wobbly. When had I last eaten? Or slept? Who knew?

Owen reached for me and pulled me into the call room. He pulled the blanket in the cot back and motioned me to get under it. I sat on the end of the bed instead and put my head between my knees, trying to get the black spots in front of my eyes to disappear. He came and crouched in front of me and started stroking my hair. I sat up quickly, almost knocking his hand away.

"Okay," he smiled. "I am a nice guy, you know. I can see you're too tired, so I'll let you off the hook. In fact, I'm going to drive you home."

"No," I argued. "Thanks but no. I'm just going to rest here for a second and then I'll walk."

"No can do," said Owen, holding my arm and lifting me up from the bed. "We need to get you home." And home sounded like such a great place to be that I let him lead me out of the room and into the parkade.

The drive home was short. I gave him directions and we were there quickly. At my door he stopped and turned off the car. He shifted in his seat so he could put his right hand behind me. "I can see you're really struggling." Then he leaned forward and put his left hand on my knee. "I can help, you know. You don't have to do this all alone."

I tried to get up, but he moved his hand further up my thigh and dug his fingers in. "I like this hard-to-get thing. It turns me on. But it's time for you to start playing along. I'm getting impatient." He moved his hand further up my leg, almost touching my most private place.

My arm swung out at him before I could stop it. He grabbed it and smiled. "You're coming to my place tomorrow."

I stared out the windshield, unable to move, but refusing to look at him. "No. No, I am not."

He smiled, and then looked down at me like I was a sweet but stupid child. "As far as everyone knows, you're practically failing this rotation. Olsen hates you, and loves me. She listens to me and will follow my recommendations. You fail this; you can kiss any decent residency goodbye. And then how will you pay those student loans? What are you in for now, sixty thousand? A hundred? And the real beauty of a medical degree is that it is COMPLETELY USELESS unless you become a doctor. It won't get you a job anywhere else. So, seven years of university, a hundred grand in debt? Bankrupt and no future. At, like, what are you, twenty-four? Big price to pay." He let his voice drift off.

He put his hands back in his lap, relaxed and confident again. "So, you're going to do this little thing for me, and I'm going to do this little thing for you, and everything is going to end up being A-Okay."

I got out of his car and stumbled to the door of my apartment building. My hands were shaking so badly it took three attempts to get the key into the lock.

Once I was inside, I quickly locked the door and then tried to slow my breathing down. I dumped my bag and coat on the floor.

In the kitchen I tried to choke back some crackers, just to get my blood sugar back up. I drank some juice, but it burned my throat and churned around in my stomach.

I needed to wash the hospital and Owen off of me. I turned the shower on hot and tried to stand up in it. I was too weak, too exhausted, so I slumped to the ground and sat under the water pounding down on me. I washed my hair and tried not to think of Liam. But every time my hand ran over my skin, every drop of water, every time bubbles slid over a sensitive place, I was back to that day: his hands massaging my breasts in the slippery soapy water, his hands between my legs, rubbing me, nearly lifting me off the ground with the pressure and strength of his touch. And the explosions of pleasure that followed when he used his tongue in my folds to lick and suck me until I sobbed and screamed.

And how we had just lain together for hours, and the rhythm of his breathing relaxed me and made me feel less alone.

I got out of the shower. I couldn't stand it. Every time I remembered him it made the present seem even worse. I had enough to cope with. There was no room for him, not even memories of him, in my life now. I wasn't sure how I was going to survive. Whenever I thought of him, the despair threatened to swamp my already sinking boat. I had let myself be open and vulnerable, and I had paid the price. I was still paying the price.

I had no more tears for Liam. He had to die in my head. No more softness. No more trips down memory lane. They left me weakened, almost destroyed. I had given someone a precious part of me, and it had meant nothing to him. Well, that should teach me. How many times was I going to have to learn this lesson?

Even worse were the times when I felt such anger towards him that, in my daydreams, I sometimes started slapping and hitting him. I didn't have the physical or mental resources left to cope with missing Liam Mason. I was on my own. I wrapped my memories of him in concrete and pushed them way back, deep into the corners of my mind, where they couldn't come out to torture me anymore. I banished him.

I dried off enough to get my pajamas on. I put a towel on my pillow to soak up the water from my wet hair. I set my alarm for 5:30am, and lay down. I was afraid I would toss and turn, but sometimes, when we really need it to be, the mind can be kind, and I was asleep in seconds.

CHAPTER TWENTY-SEVEN

In the morning, I had just hit the snooze button on my alarm when I got this text from Owen:

See you tonight. Have a shower after work, and don't forget to shave.

God, he was disgusting. His arrogance made my insides crawl. And then, in case I had forgotten, he texted:

Final review with Olsen tomorrow.

There are days in your life when, before you have even really opened your eyes you are imagining the day is finished and you are back in bed. This was one of those days for me.

In the morning I had a written exam, one of our final exams for that rotation. Despite everything going on, I had somehow managed to study enough and I thought it went all right. It was a long exam, hundreds of questions. Although I was stressed out and exhausted, I managed to stay focused. I needed to concentrate hard, which was great, because I didn't want my mind to wander too much. Dealing with one huge problem at a time had become my new survival skill and life mantra.

I was hoping that my subconscious would somehow work out a plan to save me from the Rat that evening, but by lunch nothing had appeared, and my panic was rising.

I used that nervous energy to motivate a quick study session with some of the other students on my rotation. They were a nice group of people and I regretted that we hadn't had much time together.

INVITATION

In the afternoon we had patient exams. Fake patients pretended to have illnesses or problems, and we had to interview them, examine them and discuss a plan with them. Nine times. Three an hour for three hours. I went into one room, worked with the patient, the bell went "ding" when time was up and I moved into the next room.

I had spent a lot of time with the kids and their parents, so I wasn't too worried about the whole bedside manner part of things, but the cases were often bizarre, off-the-wall diagnoses which tested more my ability to memorize the least likely of illnesses than to treat real-life children. Still, I didn't think I had actually failed any of them.

Owen the Rat was in charge of compiling all the results, but he couldn't really threaten me with that. I was allowed to request to see the examiners' comments and marks, and I would if my results were really low. It was the one place I didn't have to worry about his interference.

The day passed by. Ten hours down. Maybe eight more to go before I was back in bed? How much could happen in eight hours? Tick tick tick.

By 4:30pm, neither my conscious nor my subconscious brain had come up with a way for me to get out of dealing with Owen. Could I go to Dr. Olsen? No, she seemed to think he was God's gift to medicine. Could I go to my faculty advisor? It was a no-win there. The year before, another female resident had gone to talk to someone about her research boss who was putting the moves on her. He denied it, of course, and said she was simply a woman scorned. He said she had tried to bribe him for a better mark, and when he turned her down, she tried to attack his reputation. Somebody's reputation was destroyed that day, but it wasn't his.

The whole situation was taking me back to the dark days after the incident, when my heart and body was battered, and my future seemed empty. I felt dirty and worthless again. The despair moved over me like a black cloud and I had trouble thinking straight. I didn't feel much of anything. Numb, I guess. Maybe that was a protective thing, or maybe I had just really given up.

What did I have if I screwed this up? No family. No money. No career. Worse than no career, because crippling student loans would make it so I could never go back to school again, and what school or employer wasn't going to think twice about someone who had made it halfway through medical school and then suddenly flunked out, or dropped out?

I was just one small person drowning alone in a dark world. There was no one to pull me out but myself.

I could refuse to spend time with Owen and let him fail me. But that would just keep me in his clutches for another three months. I would just end up back at this point all over again.

I realized then that there must be something innately wrong with me. I did bring on these terrible things. I did somehow attract these awful people with their sick attentions. Chloe and my father were right. I didn't know how to just keep my head down and get on with things.

I took a deep breath, and I just gave up. I would let whatever had to happen, happen. I would make myself pretty and offer myself up on a plate to the person with the power. I would leave my body and go far away until it was finished. Then I would get up the next day and never, ever think of it again.

CHAPTER TWENTY-EIGHT

As I walked home I got another message from Owen:
I'll pick you up at 7pm. Wear something nice.
That gave me enough time to shower. And shave. I tried to
get clean, to smell nice. I found a pretty dress from the days before The Incident. I guessed I was going to have to start referring
to it as The First Incident after the coming night with Owen. I
didn't have the energy to laugh at the dark humor.

I checked myself over in the mirror. I felt no connection at
all to the body staring back at me. It was a mannequin I was
looking over, checking to see that it would meet Owen's approval. Pretty makeup, check. Tight but classy dress, check. My
precious, special black lingerie, check.

The surface of me was wrapped up like a shiny present. But
inside was rotten, dark, polluted and ruined.

I waited for Owen outside my building. I leaned against the
stucco, running my hands roughly along it. The wind was cold,
with slivers of icy rain. It felt cool on my skin and I liked that it
hurt. It was the perfect weather for how I felt.

Owen pulled up, leaned across the car's interior and pushed
the door open. I walked over and got in.

"You look gooood." He wore the grin of a predator. I
smiled back. The new me said, "Nice car." I ran my hand sug-
gestively along the dashboard. "Very sexy."

"I know, right?" He relaxed, enjoying this turn of events.
I'm sure he was expecting more of a fight from me. Maybe he

even wanted one, who knows? But he wasn't going to get it. I was finished with me. He could take whatever he wanted.

He placed his hand on me knee, and we drove along in silence. I let the passing view of the dark grey city numb me even further.

We pulled onto a pretty street and into the driveway of a new townhouse. "It's mine." Owen looked to me for approval.

"Nice." I nodded and gave a little smile. I decided to just leave the fake smile on my face. It was easier that way.

We walked up the stairs to the door. He buzzed some numbers. The door opened and we went in. I looked around and gave him another smile, because that was what I was supposed to do.

It was a nice enough room. Very bachelor-ish of course. The new style of dark hardwood, steel kitchen, brown leather couch, giant black TV. I liked it the way I had liked the weather. It suited my mood. I fit right in here.

"Take your coat off," he ordered. I hesitated a bit, which I saw excited him. I wasn't sure yet how to play the game. Taunt him a little? I didn't have the energy to play hard to get. Why pretend? He had the power. We both knew it.

I removed my coat and dropped it onto the floor beside me. I went to take off my heels, but he said, "No, baby. Leave those on."

He went to sit in the living room. "Come here."

I did as he said and stood in the doorway. "No, come where I can see you." He gestured in front of the chair he was sitting in. "I want to look at you until I can't take it anymore."

I stood in from of him. "Look in my eyes". I did, but my vision blurred and I went farther away. He sat back in his chair and stared. His hard-on became obvious. I was trying to get myself to go to him, but my body wouldn't move. My brain was snapping commands, "Go over there. Touch him. Get this done. Faster is better." But my body wouldn't do it. I stood as still as a stone.

He stood instead and walked to me. He stroked my hair, almost gently. He cupped his hand around my neck and said,

INVITATION

"Thank you so much for coming." I think he honestly believed I had come just because he was so desirable. There was some whole new kind of crazy going on in that room.

He put his hands on either side of my face, and pulled me forward onto his lips. My body trembled and I couldn't kiss him back.

"Too fast?" He smiled. He moved his hands slowly down my shoulders, then inward until his thumbs grazed my nipples. He rubbed then gently. My dress wrapped around the front, and he pushed the material back exposing more of my neck and chest. He kissed my skin as he rubbed my nipples.

My brain kept repeating, "Just do this. This is who you are. You are bad and ruined, so what's this one more thing?" But my body was having trouble accepting it all. I had to swallow down the waves of nausea that kept rising.

He lifted the skirt of my dress, and put his hand between my thighs. My legs clamped shut, beyond my control. This excited him, and he laughed deeply. His hand began to move up.

CHAPTER TWENTY-NINE

Suddenly I heard a small noise coming from another room. "What's that?" I stepped back from him.

He pulled me closer again, and said, laughing, "That's dessert."

Shock and fear propelled me away from him, toward the room. In the doorway, I flicked on the light. It was his bedroom. A young woman was on the bed, shielding her eyes from the bright light. There was something very familiar about her, but my mind couldn't quite work it out.

"Hi," she waved slowly. Everything about her was slow: her speech, her smile, her movements.

"Is she high?" I turned to Owen.

"I gave her something to relax." Owen looked at her and they both laughed. "Isn't that right, baby?" To me he said, "She was nervous about it being the three of us tonight."

She shrugged, and looked even younger than she had at first appeared. Owen moved to sit beside her on the bed. He grabbed her breast and twisted it. She cried out and slapped his hand away.

He grabbed a fist of her hair. "But you're just a dirty, little thing aren't you?" He used his grip on her hair to move her head up and down, nodding. She pouted and tried to pull away, but she was too weak. I stared at her face, and suddenly knew exactly where I had seen her.

It woke me up. I was back in my body, enraged and strong and thinking clearly. Those men had called me dirty and disgusting, and I had believed it. They had done filthy things to my body and then twisted it all around so that I was somehow the disgusting one. Even my own father had said I was worthless, and I had believed him, too.

But in front of me was a woman, a child, who was lovely and worthy and who should have a whole life of good moments and love ahead of her. Beside her was a rotten person, perverse, manipulative and corrupt. How wrong, how sick that anyone could look at a scene like this and think that the girl had deserved or asked to be treated as though she had no value at all.

I wanted to pick up the table lamp and smash it into the back of Owen's head. My arms wanted to rip him off the bed and away from her, but my mind had come back, finally, to help.

"I want to take pictures," I said in my softest, most sultry voice. I needed to sound turned on. "I'm going to get my phone."

I hurried back to the front entrance, to grab my purse. I scrambled to find the phone and moved quickly back into his bedroom. By the time I got there, the girl was nearly passed out, and he had undone her top. She was braless, and her open shirt exposed her breasts.

"You next," he said, gesturing towards the bed.

"You first." I purred. "It'll make me hot to see you."

He smiled and moved off the bed. "Undress me, then," he sneered. I was happy to do it. I brushed my hands along his neck and chest as I removed his shirt. I couldn't bring myself to touch him anywhere below the waist, but I looked into his eyes, smiled, and licked my lips as his pants and then his underwear dropped to the floor.

"Get on the bed." I said. He practically jumped onto it. "Lay down beside her." I took out my phone and started taking pictures. "Oh, this is so sexy." He was completely naked and hard as a rock. He was clearly proud of all his physical attributes, and pleased by my attention.

I emailed the pictures to myself as soon as they were taken.

He started touching himself. "Come here." I took more pictures, pretending to laugh and enjoy myself. He was growing impatient. "Come here now," he growled.

I put my camera back in my purse, tucked my hair behind my ears and said, "No. That's not going to happen."

He laughed, like it was a game, but his face clouded over. He was about to bark more orders at me.

"I've seen her in the Outpatient clinic," I told him.

For a split second he looked nervous, but quickly covered it up. "Yeah, so. I met her there."

"Not really supposed to be dating patients, are we?" He glared at me. "Might be worth mentioning to your supervisor? Or the Physician's College?"

He looked confident again. "She's just the aunt of some kid. Okay, it's not ideal. But I'm not exactly going to lose my license over dating some kid's relative. I'll say I didn't know."

He thought he had me. He sprang across the room, grabbed my arm and started dragging me towards the bed.

I ripped my arm away. "She is NOT the patient's Aunt," I snarled between gritted teeth. He shrugged. "She is his SISTER, and she is SIXTEEN years old!"

Owen froze. He glared at me and looked ready to argue. But then he looked down at the girl. She had fallen asleep, or passed out, and with her face soft and vulnerable she looked more like she was twelve. His hands started to shake.

He stood and came towards me. He snatched at my bag, trying to grab the camera. I took it out and offered it to him. "Feel free. I've already sent the pictures."

He shoved my hand away and snapped, "Hey, she told me she was older." I backed away from him. "It could happen to anybody! She's just a little slut!"

I slapped him hard across the face. "Don't you EVER call anyone that again." I glared at him. He looked frightened, and I was glad. "Her name is Isabel, you ass. Call us a cab!" He started to protest. "Now!"

He ran from the room. I moved toward Isabel and started doing up her clothes. I moved her head around, trying to wake her a little, and her eyes finally opened. She tried to focus on me. "We're getting out of here, sweetie." She nodded. "I need you to try to stand up."

She was tiny. My body was coursing with anger and rage, and I had plenty of power to help move her little body towards the door. How could anyone have thought she was nineteen?

There were opaque windows along the sides of the door, and we stood there waiting for the outline of a taxi to show up. It did, finally, and I began unlocking the door. Owen ran towards us, and the look in his eyes, the fear and the hatred that was there, frightened me. I struggled with the chain and then the deadbolt. I was trying to keep Isabel upright while pushing us both out the door.

Owen was begging and trying to shut the door on us. "You just have to hear me out," he yelled over and over. I shoved him aside, and pushed Isabel and myself through the door. It was dark outside and I was watching the steps to make sure we didn't fall.

I ran straight into a man and screamed in fear. I jumped back, eyes wide open. It was Liam. He had his arms raised. He looked alarmed and confused. His eyes swept back and forth from Isabel to me, trying to figure out what was happening. He looked up the steps. Owen stood watching, pale as a ghost. He slammed the door closed and bolted the locks.

The driver of the cab opened his door and got out, but stayed well back of the trouble. "Everything, okay, miss? You want me to call the police?"

"No," I answered him, starting to move toward the car. "We need a ride."

Liam grabbed at my arm, "Madison. Honey. What's going on?" He tried to smile. He really had no idea what had happened. He said, jokingly, "I came to rescue you."

I stared him down, trying to bring my breathing under control. "I rescued myself, you asshole." My voice was so cold and hard I didn't recognize it.

He moved towards me, opening his arms for an embrace. With my free arm I punched him hard in the chest. I backed away and glared at him. "Get away from us. Get away!" I know I sounded hysterical, but everything was boiling up in me at once. "I don't ever want to see you again! You heartless asshole!! Fuck you!!" My voice was hoarse and cracking from screaming. "FUCK. YOU!!"

I dragged Isabel into the cab and told the driver to take us to the hospital. I didn't even look back as we pulled away.

CHAPTER THIRTY

When we got to the hospital, I took Isabel to the cafeteria. She was coming around, and ordered a soda and some fries. I asked permission to look through her purse and found her phone. "Your Mom in here?" I asked.

"Sure," she answered. "Just scroll down to 'Home'.

What magical words those were. Mom. Home.

I talked to Isabel's Mom, Marie. I asked her to meet us at the hospital. She was there in thirty minutes, confused and distressed. I told her what I knew, and that she could take Isabel into Emerg to have a rape kit done. They would take samples in case charges were pressed.

"Did that happen?!" Marie was distraught. She couldn't bring herself to say rape. She looked to me for answers.

I wanted to reassure her, but I didn't want her to sweep this under the rug. Isabel needed to be examined. "I didn't see anything like that. But I don't know for sure. She was already there when I arrived."

We looked at Isabel, who shrugged. She didn't know either.

"What should we do?" Marie asked me.

"Take her to see the doctor. Talk about it. Maybe call a lawyer. It'll be up to you and Isabel where to go from here."

I stood to leave. Marie stood and came towards me. She wrapped her arms around me. "Thank you, honey," she murmured into my neck.

She held onto me for a long time.

I walked home, beyond exhausted. I guess I wasn't numb anymore because it seemed like a lifetime of pain rose up to swallow me. I was trying not to start crying, because I could tell it was going to be bad. Awful. The kind of sobbing where you feel like your mind and your body are breaking. I needed to get home.

I walked as fast as I could and reached my apartment quickly. I was unlocking the door when I heard footsteps behind me. I spun around, terrified.

It was Liam. My beautiful Liam. And seeing him there, lost to me, made me realize I had loved him. The pain had been so great because he had meant so much. Too much. But never again.

I didn't trust myself to talk. My chin was quivering with the effort of not crying. So I shook my head and turned away from him. He moved forward, slowly and spoke gently, "Maddie. You're scaring me." He moved toward me, but I just backed away resigned. It was all over.

"You can't be alone right now."

A horribly bitter laugh came out of me. Why not? I was always alone. It was time to just adapt. Harden up and get on with things, like everybody else seemed to do.

He held the door open for me and said, "I'm coming in."

I shrugged. It didn't matter. I couldn't say anything without crying, and I wasn't going to break down in front of this person.

We walked down the hall to my door, together but apart. I opened the door and dumped my coat and purse on the floor. I kicked them out of my way. I looked up at Liam, expecting his to be evaluating my outfit, my body, but his eyes were looking right into mine. I turned away. He followed me, a devoted shadow. I took my hair down and washed my face. He tried to catch my eyes in the mirror -- I could see his shy smile out of the corner of my eye -- but I moved past him into my room. I left him standing in the hallway and shut the door.

I took all my clothes off, and got into my warmest sweats. I gathered up my dress, my tights, and my fancy lingerie. I carried it through my apartment and out into the hallway. I dumped it all down the garbage chute.

I went back inside, ignoring Liam completely. I was shaking with cold. I pulled extra blankets out of the cupboard and got into bed. I was never going to be warm again.

I didn't have the energy for a scene with Liam. That would have to wait. The energy required to force him to leave was beyond me.

I wasn't worried about having him in my house. He would never hurt me -- physically. He was the kindest, gentlest asshole I'd ever met.

As soon as I thought it, I started crying. I curled myself into a tiny ball in the center of my bed. I saw the door open a crack, letting light in from the hallway. I tried to say, "Get out," but only managed to produce a desperate sob, which started a whole new wave of crying.

Liam came and sat by the side of the bed. My hands were curled up under my chin. He curled his strong hands around my smaller ones. I couldn't pull away. My body loved his touched, no secret there. Getting rid of him was a battle my heart and head were going to have to wage, and it wasn't going to happen that night.

And, if I'm being completely honest, I just couldn't make him let go of me. The warmth and strength of his fingers wrapped around mine was probably the greatest comfort I'd ever had. It was too hard to pull away.

I fell into sleep.

CHAPTER THIRTY-ONE

I expected to wake up the next day feeling terrible, but I didn't. I was still physically wiped out, after all, I had slept only 6 hours; but my body felt light and my mind was calm.

That lasted about five minutes, and then the reality of the day I was facing hit me. It slammed me down into the bed. So much had happened, and there was so much left to deal with. I wasn't sure how to make it through exactly, but staying in bed wasn't going to help the situation.

From my point of view, I had three main issues going on. Number one: Tell Liam he had to go. For good. Number two: Get my evaluation from Dr. Olsen, and deal with whatever fall-out there would be from that. And number three: If Isabel had decided what to do about Owen, I would probably need to help out there in some way, too.

After that, I had two blissful days off, during which I planned to sleep and eat healthy things and drink various brightly colored juices in order to build my system back up. The last three months had been, excuse my language, a real bitch.

Armed with something of a plan, I swung out of bed and grabbed my robe. It was about 6am, still dark and rainy out.

I walked toward the kitchen, hoping to find my phone somewhere along the way. I thought I had left it in my coat, which I had dumped on the floor when I dragged my exhausted self in the day before. I expected there to be some short text from Liam, to which I would reply, well, I didn't really know. I had cared so much for him. I hadn't admitted it to myself, but I had started to think of us as more than physical friends. I had started to imagine a future.

But he had made plans with me, and then just dumped me. By text. So long, sister, and then not a word. He hadn't even responded when I'd pretty much begged for help with Owen. It had been a big deal, a huge deal, for me to try to get over those other men, to give Liam a chance to show me he was a good man. But, no, they were all the same.

Still, if I expected a big fight from my heart and my body, I was wrong. He hadn't left the night before. As I came around the corner, I saw Liam asleep on the couch.

When I saw him there, gorgeously disheveled, seemingly full of concern, I felt . . . I felt nothing. Nothing at all. It was like there was a stranger sitting in my living room. I was so relieved I almost laughed out loud. This was going to be so easy. I would cut him out of my life, swear off men for a few more years, and get back to focusing on school and work.

He was awake at that point, and he stood, dropping my extra blanket onto the floor. He took a few steps towards me. "Are you okay? Are we okay? Can I give you a hug?"

I took a step back and walked into the kitchen. "We are fine, and no you may not give me a hug. You have to go."

"Can you at least tell me what happened last night? I was so worried, I am so worried about you."

So, I made tea while he used the bathroom and tried to tidy up enough for work. When he came back we sat at the tiny table and ate cereal. I told him about Owen and the threats, and about Isabel. His jaw clenched and he slapped his hand down on the table. "I'll kill him."

I had no patience for him. "Oh, save it, Caveman. I've got this." I was tired of the bravado and the bullshit. Where were these guys when you really needed them? I'd had enough.

There were some things I was curious about, though. "Why did you go to Owen's house, anyway?" I asked.

"I talked to your nurse pal on the ward and she told me that Owen had been giving you a hard time. Then she told me she saw him driving you home once. I know what kind of guy he is. It doesn't take a rocket scientist to figure out that something was wrong. When I couldn't find you at the hospital or your place, I thought I'd better try Owen's."

"What do you mean, 'what kind of guy he is'?"

"He's a jerk. He says terrible things about women. He's just a pig. Let's leave it at that."

I shrugged. What did I care what Liam wanted and didn't want to talk about. I started clearing away the bowls and mugs. He took them to the sink and started rinsing them. I snatched them away. "No, you don't get to show up here and start acting all domesticated. You were right all along. This can't work. I don't want this to work."

I walked to the door to put on my old coat and my trustworthy boots. Liam hurried to keep up. "Can I walk with you?"

I sighed. I didn't want him to, but it seemed like it would take more effort to refuse. "Fine."

We went down the hall of the apartment building and pushed the squeaky old door open. Outside, the rain continued on. This time, though, I had my umbrella.

As I opened the umbrella, it nearly poked Liam's eye out. I was at exactly the wrong (or right) height to cause bodily damage. So he took the umbrella and held it over both of us. In order to keep us dry, his body was pressed up against mine. Three weeks ago it would have been thrilling. Now it was just a nuisance. I kept tripping on his feet. I could tell he was hoping it would make me laugh, and that that would lighten the mood.

But that didn't happen, it would never happen. I couldn't be with him anymore. It wasn't safe. I would fall hard for this guy and he would hurt me badly. I had no one but myself to pick me up when he inevitably crushed me, and I had so much to lose if I fell apart. I considered the whole "incident" of my time with Liam to be a good warning. It had been terrible, but I had survived. No more risks for me, though. I was just too tired.

His hands were clenching and he looked like he was trying really hard to say something. "Look, this is not a great time to talk…" I nodded in agreement and continued along. He grasped my arm and pulled me to a stop.

"I made a huge mistake. I miss you so much. Can we please just try this thing?" He put his hand on the side of my face and I moved away.

I shook my head. "Why bother? You were right. It's doomed, so why prolong the agony?"

"It's not doomed if we say it's not."

"Yeah, but what will happen is that we'll say it's not, then you'll change your mind, and I'll end up devastated, alone, and barely functional. You'll go back to one of your two lovely bachelor pads, with all your buddies for support, and your Mom and Dad to pick up the pieces."

He pulled me closer. He moved in to kiss me and I let him. I guess he thought this was going to be like Snow White or something and he'd thaw me with his kiss. The thing is, he had already used that trick and, for me at least, this was no fairy tale.

He stood back and looked in my face. His shoulders slumped in disappointment at my lack of response; but soon he stood up straight and handed me the umbrella. As he headed towards the entrance of the hospital, he looked back at me. "I think you almost loved me once. I think I love you. I'm not giving up, Madison. Life is short and you're too special. I'm going to make you love me."

Good luck with that, I thought.

CHAPTER THIRTY-TWO

In the interest of full disclosure, my lips did tingle, slightly, from that kiss.

Still, I had a meeting with Dr. Olsen to get through so it was fairly easy to turn my mind from Liam. I had morning rounds to do first, for the last time. As happy as I was to, hopefully, be getting away from the Pediatrics unit, it was sad to be seeing those little faces for the last time.

I was especially saddened to see Alex back in the hospital. I flipped through his chart and saw that he now had pneumonia. Poor kid couldn't catch a break. I went to see him and was dismayed. He was pale and even skinnier. He had an oxygen mask on, and three different IV's going. He gave me a weak smile.

"Hey, kiddo." I touched his hand gently. "How're you holding up?"

He shrugged, too tired or too fed up to smile. "Why are there so many doctors around here?" he accused.

I shook my head. "I don't know. What do you mean"?

"That other guy was here. The one who likes you."

I'm sure my face fell. "Dr. Humphries."?

He rolled his eyes. "No, not that dork. The nice one. Dr. Mason."

"I'm not sure. Maybe he's on Pediatrics now. Some of us are changing rotations tomorrow."

"I don't think so. He admitted me from Emerg."

I can't tell you for sure if my heart sank in despair or flipped in joy. I was scheduled to start an Emergency rotation the following week and had counted on Liam still being at the other hospital.

We talked a few minutes more. Alex figured that we probably didn't have to say a real good-bye since I'd likely see him in Emergency from time to time. As humor went it was a little dark, but it was also likely to be true. I liked that he could see some silver lining to all his future admissions.

As I was leaving, he piped up, "So, is Dr. Mason your boyfriend?"

I was taken aback by this tiny boy's astuteness, wondering what adult vibes he had picked up on.

"Why do you ask?"

"Because you're both nice. And you both wear lab coats."

So there you go. The wisdom of childhood. If only it stayed that simple and easy. I smiled at him and waved good-bye.

It was creeping up on 10am, time to face the ogre. I couldn't say what was going to happen. Would Owen still try to blackball me? Would he come out fighting? Cornered rats often do.

I walked over to the teaching area where a lot of the doctors have their offices. Dr. Olsen was waiting for me, reading something intently. She looked as grumpy as ever. Super.

"Have a seat, Madison." I did as she said, but couldn't get comfortable. I stayed perched on the edge of the chair. Flight or fight, I guess.

"I'm perplexed," she started. I waited. "I have your review from your chief resident, Dr. Humphries." She looked up at me, but I kept my face blank. "It is not a good evaluation." She looked up again, but I held my tongue. I didn't know what I should say. Telling her what had happened seemed like a good way to get myself into a lawsuit if I made Owen look bad at work. If he denied everything and Isabel refused to talk, then I really had no ground to stand on.

It was back to the "he said, she said" business. The unfairness being, of course, that the people in power get to do whatever they want to you, and then people believe the people in power because, obviously, they're the people in power. I waited.

"Which doesn't make a lot of sense to me, to be honest." Now I looked up and made eye contact with her.

"I found you to be very diligent. Your exam marks improved every time, and the nurses say you were wonderful to work with and great with the kids and their parents. Which is something, because I find most of the parents annoying as hell." Was Dr. Olsen making a joke? I couldn't tell until she looked up at me, a small smile on her face.

I was expecting a big discussion, a huge fight with tremendous repercussions; but instead she just tossed Owen's assessment into the shredder. "Sometimes I have to overlook these residents' opinions. I can only assume he was very sleep-deprived."

I could barely speak I was so shocked. Could it really be that someone, some adult, was being a professional, was doing her job? Could it be that Owen had been so delusional about his ability to influence her opinion? Well, of course, that part was possible. The guy was nuts. "Thank you," was all I could think to say.

"You're welcome. If you need a reference later on come find me." I started to thank her again, but she switched right back into grump mode, flicked her wrist at me and said, "You can go now." I did, before she could change her mind.

CHAPTER THIRTY-THREE

I looked down at my phone and saw a text from Liam. He wanted to meet me in the cafeteria. I'm not sure why I agreed. I'm going to blame my good mood and ravenous hunger.

The cafeteria in our hospital is not the typical brown paneling, linoleum nightmare of many hospitals. The furniture is boring, but not horrible. There are lots of windows, and sunlight, as with most places, helps to make it look almost cheerful.

But what truly made the cafeteria look great that day was Liam. Holy god that man was beautiful. Gorgeous, yet approachable, strong like an athlete, but not artificially pumped up and vain. His smile lit up the whole room, and I can't deny that it lit me up, too.

But I had to stick to my guns. The stronger my reaction to him now, the worse it would be again when he hurt me. It's some sort of direct equation. The greater the appeal, the greater the despair. I might write a book about it.

I was curious, though. "What are we doing here, Liam?"

He patted the seat next to him and I sat down. He leaned in to me and my whole body responded. Against the wishes of my brain, I leaned a little toward him, too.

"I need to talk to you. Last night was no good for talking."

"Why is today any better?"

"Because I can see you're doing all right. I thought you'd be a mess." I must have given him a sharp look, because he quickly added, "You have every right to be a wreck. That was a bad scene. It's still a bad scene." He crumpled a napkin in his hands. I found the nervousness a little bit endearing. "What's going to happen with Isabel?"

"I don't know." I sighed. "And I don't want to talk about it here. Too many ears, and I don't want to get upset at work. You know."

"Sure. So, can we talk about something else?"

I hesitated, but eventually nodded.

"I need to see you. I have some things to say to you. I want to tell you why I didn't call you back."

"Didn't call me back?!" I tried to keep my voice down, but I was angry. "We made three weeks' worth of plans. You say you want to spend every spare minute with me, and then you stand me up. Then you break up with me. In. A. Text . . .Then you don't answer, like three messages from me . . ."

"Four," he interrupted. My glare silenced him.

I'd lost steam and momentum, though, by the time I said, "When you left, it nearly took me down, Liam. I can't take any more risks like that. There's no one to pick me up when I fall."

"I could be." He reached for my hand and, much as I would have liked to just grab onto it, I pulled away. I stood to go. "We're so good together."

"No," I argued. "Our bodies are good together. That's it, and it's not enough. I don't want to be with anyone right now. And when I do try again, I'll be looking for a person with a heart."

He pulled me gently back down to sit beside him. "I have a heart. I cared so much for you, I got scared."

I think I rolled my eyes like Alex. "Hey," Liam was suddenly angry. "You're not the only one with 'issues', okay? Was I a jerk about the stuff with those guys, and Chloe?"

He had me there. He had been shockingly mature and kind. "No, you were not a jerk. You were great."

"So you don't get to be a jerk about my stuff. I know it's stupid, but you could at least hear me out."

Which seemed fair. "All right." I stood up once more. "But I'm all drama'd out. I'm taking tomorrow off. Can we meet on Sunday?"

He stood up to walk me to the elevators. "It's a date, mademoiselle."

I wasn't sure what it was exactly, but I didn't argue.

CHAPTER THIRTY-FOUR

I met up with the other interns from my rotation to compare notes on our evaluations and our upcoming assignments.

As I said, I was starting Emergency the following Monday. I hadn't asked Liam if he would be at the same hospital I would. I wasn't sure what answer I wanted to hear.

The other interns and I ate a long lunch, the first in three months, and went our separate ways. We each had another Orientation to get to. I couldn't help but think back to the one for Peds, and the glimpse I'd caught of Liam and what I had wanted to do with his hair . . .

I was blushing furiously, as well as starting to ache in my sensitive spots (Isn't 'erogenous zone' the least erogenous phrase you've ever heard?) I shook my head to snap myself out of it.

The interns starting in Emergency were meeting in the small north atrium. I looked around quickly, praying that Chloe wasn't there. She wasn't supposed to be on this rotation, but it wasn't impossible to switch. I didn't see her, though, which was an enormous relief.

There are tables and chairs in the atrium, but by the time I got there it was standing room only. I leaned against the wall on my right, facing forward to see the speaker. I was trying to look enthusiastic and semi-intelligent, but the last few days were catching up with me.

I hadn't had much sleep; I'd been through an emotional wringer. I had gone through an evaluation I had been dreading for months. Of course I was happy it had gone well, but even happiness and relief can be exhausting. Or maybe it was just the fact that I had actually eaten an entire meal without rushing off in the middle of it to resuscitate a patient (or Owen's ego) that caused me to feel so sleepy and relaxed. I tried not to close my eyes or yawn.

I felt a tickle on my neck as the air behind me moved. Once again, I didn't even need to turn around to know it with him. Liam. My Liam. Damn him. Would I always think of him as my Liam, even when I was old and grey and hadn't seen him for fifty years? And why did I even think of him that way at all? He had obviously NEVER been my Liam, and I hadn't meant enough to him to even warrant a text back.

Screw you Liam, I was thinking, as he put a hand on my upper arm and squeezed. Then he walked away. The skin his fingers had pressed would tingle and burn for the rest of the day. I couldn't tell if I had been touched by an angel or a devil. Maybe both.

The rest of the day went by slowly. At the end, some of the interns asked me to go out to dinner with them. I was so tired, but I thought I needed to make more friends. My loner life was growing old, and if I couldn't have love and intimacy and romance, then at least I could have cheap beer, chicken wings, and a few laughs.

I barely remember dropping into bed at 9pm. That day was done. Hallelujah.

CHAPTER THIRTY-FIVE

I woke the next morning to the incessant buzz of my apartment's call bell.

I ignored it.

I ignored it some more.

Finally my phone started ringing as well, at which point I lurched out of bed muttering obscenities under my breath. I picked up the phone to check the number. Liam.

"I said Sunday. I said I was resting today. No drama." I hung up. Dramatically. Damn!

It rang again. I answered, and Liam quickly butted in, "Let me up. I just need a second."

So, I wrapped my comfortable old robe around me and went to brush my teeth. I wasn't going to put any effort into my appearance at that moment, but there were still basic items of personal hygiene to attend to.

It was taking a while for Liam to get to my apartment. I heard a racket further down the hall, then Liam's face popped into view.

"Go back in." He shooed me backwards. "I have a surprise for you." I tilted my head in a "You've got to be kidding," pose, but he was having none of it. He came and pushed me back into my apartment. Then he kept gently pushing me until I was back in my bedroom.

"Okay, enough! What are you doing?" I demanded.

"Just go back to bed. I have some stuff to do out here."

INVITATION

Remarkable as it may seem, I actually did go back to bed and closed my eyes. I had slept so well, but felt even more tired than before. It was like my body suddenly remembered what sleep felt like, and how little it had been getting. Now it was demanding much more of it.

There was a lot of banging around going on. I couldn't imagine what he was doing. Setting up a treadmill? What the hell?

Finally, he appeared at my door.

"Are you awake now or should I come back later?"

I glanced at my clock. In fairness to Liam, it was 10am. He hadn't really appeared at the crack of dawn. It just felt that way.

"No, I'm awake. Sort of." I started to get up.

"Okay. Great. First you need to put this on." He clutched a tiny pile of fabric in his hand.

"On what?"

He smiled and began straightening out the cloth. He held the pieces up.

"Underwear?" I started to go back to bed.

"Bathing suit," he offered.

"First of all, that's not a bathing suit. It's a pile of leftover yarn. And secondly, have you lost your ever-loving mind? It's pouring rain. In Seattle. In early April."

"Come on. Humor me." He handed over the suit. "It'll fit. I told the clerk all about you."

I imagined him holding up his hands to some woman, trying to explain my cup size. It made me smile, and I took pity on him. I reached for the bikini.

"Okay. I'll wait in the living room."

I put the suit on. It was a bikini, like something from a Sports Illustrated cover. Bits of turquoise string connected to other bits of turquoise string. I suddenly thought of the dream I had had recently. My lower abdomen flipped, a tiny instant orgasm.

I looked at myself in the mirror and thought I looked all right. I didn't care about impressing Liam, so it took the pressure off.

"Wow." I turned to find him in the doorway. He came toward me. "Okay, Madison. I know you're always cold, and I wish I could take you somewhere hot and tropical, so I could fight off snakes and tigers and prove my manliness..."

"I don't think your manliness has been called into question."

"Right. Heartless is my problem." I didn't answer. I didn't want to make this into some game. It hadn't been funny for me. I would let him have his say, but that was it.

He came toward me and my nipples got hard. I swear it was just the chilly air. I have no idea why my lips were throbbing or why I couldn't take my eyes off Liam's mouth.

"I think your body trusted me. And I think I can get the rest of you to trust me." He took my hand and started leading me toward the living room.

"I can't take you to Hawaii right now, because we're both hospital slaves with no holidays ever, so I brought the vacation to you."

CHAPTER THIRTY-SIX

I looked around the room and couldn't keep the delight off my face. He had brought a gorgeous reclining deck chair with a thick soft cushion. He had set it up under a heat lamp, which was gently warming the room to a delicious tropical temperature. His phone was attached to speakers and he turned it on. The relaxing sounds of waves and wind poured out, and I felt the tension leaving my body.

He pulled me to the fridge and opened it. I think I clasped my hands together and exclaimed like a child. He had filled it with my favorite things. "You're been looking so thin and pale -- no offense -- so I brought you food packed with energy and vitamins. Also juices because I know you like them. And tea, just in case you were all out."

I was amazed. And so touched. "But why? Why are you doing this?"

"Because you said you needed a rest and I thought this would help."

"But now, just to be polite, I have to ask you to stay to join me." I tried to look disapprovingly at him.

He smiled, obviously happy to see my pleasure. "I'm not staying. But I have you booked for tomorrow, and we need to discuss some serious stuff then. I want your full attention. I want you to be relaxed, and happy and fully rested."

I started pushing him gently towards the door. I couldn't wait to sit down, grab a book and just disappear for the day.

Liam had stocked me up so well that I didn't even need to go out for food. "Okay, I'm impressed. This is really nice."

"Wait!" He scrambled to remove a bottle from the pocket of his coat. "Sunscreen!"

It was actually body oil. My favorite brand. He had even noticed that.

"Why don't I just put it on you, and then I'll take off?"

I tried to say, "Forget it," but my mouth wouldn't obey my brain.

"Don't worry. I'll be quick." He was pushing his way back into the room. He wrapped his arms around my waist and lifted me up, carrying me toward the chair.

He adjusted it to lie flat and then helped me get onto it. "Flip to your stomach. I'll do your back."

Damn right, I thought. Those fingers weren't going anywhere near the front of me. What can I blame my lack of will power on? The lights that Liam dimmed, the sound of waves, the warmth, the insanely comfortable chair? It was only a massage, right?

I looked away from Liam. I placed my arms above my head so they were resting against the cushion. It really did feel as though I were lying in the sun, off on some fantastic holiday.

I couldn't see what Liam was doing, but I heard him sit down beside the chair and take the plastic cap off the oil. He rubbed it in his hands to warm it.

"Am I allowed to say you are the most beautiful woman I've ever seen?"

"No."

"I guess I'll have to show you then, instead."

He ran his hands gently down my back and legs. His strokes were soft and smooth. I felt myself drifting off. Slowly, though, the strokes became more forceful. They moved deeper into my muscles, releasing aches and knots and making me sigh with pleasure.

His hands began moving up the insides of my legs and I clamped them shut.

"We've already established that my body likes you. It's my heart and my mind that are the problems here." I kept my thigh muscles clenched, but god it was hard.

He moved closer and I felt his warm breath on the small of my back. The muscles spasmed in pleasure, arching my back and raising my pelvis up.

"Well, since your body and I are such good friends already, how about we just play for a bit while you rest."

I was already half-asleep. I felt strong enough to resist his attempts to win me over emotionally and rationally, so why not let the poor boy have some physical fun? There's really no way I can justify it. It was just me, nearly naked, under a warm sun, in the more than capable hands of the unbelievably sexy Liam. Who loved my body and wanted it to feel good.

All my muscles surrendered. He sensed the change and went back to gently stoking my inner thighs. Each stroke came closer to my aching wet center, until my breathing was becoming ragged.

"These are interfering with my massage techniques." He undid the back tie of the top of my bathing suit, and began long, deep strokes along my spine. His large strong hands moved around my waist to the front and then swooped back along the top of my ass.

He undid the ties on the sides of the bottom half of my suit and pulled it down, onto my legs. I was completely naked now, and almost paralyzed by relaxation. And pleasure.

He massaged my ass and moved lower, pressing his thumbs between my thighs. This time my legs let him part them slightly. He took my ankles and pulled my legs farther apart. I whimpered and my back arched again. My body was responding without any input from me. Liam was right. They were very good friends, whether or not I wanted to cooperate.

Liam's hands were back on my thighs, moving between them, closer and closer to where I was aching to be touched. He had awakened a longing in me that only he could fill. And he used his power so well. He pushed the bathing suit completely out of the way.

His hand started massaging a gentle circle across my bottom, which grew larger as the seconds passed. Eventually, my legs had spread themselves completely apart, my back was arching, and my pelvis and ass were pushing upwards, willing his hand downwards. I kept my face away from him. I was ashamed at my inability to keep him away. I couldn't make eye contact, or I would have to either go to him completely or make him stop. I wouldn't do either.

Finally he slipped his hand through my parted thighs. When he first touched my tender wet flesh, I gasped and he groaned. I was lost again. Only he could do this to me.

I arched up higher, opening myself to him. His fingers slid down my swollen cleft, parting my lips. He circled slowly around my clitoris. Then he stopped moving his fingers, but his thumb pushed into the soft swollen flesh of my vagina and started circling. He pushed it in and out until my hips were thrusting on their own, pressing down into the pillow for release.

"No." He grabbed my hips with his other hand, stopping their rocking. "That's my job." His voice was thick with want.

His thumb resumed its slow circling and plunging, while his fingers found my clitoris. His touch was so soft. I wanted to cry out in desperation. Instead I bit down on my hand to keep from begging.

The rubbing grew firmer, the plunging harder. Faster and faster he circled my clitoris and finally moved right onto it. I cried out and tried to move my hips, which were still pinned by Liam. He wanted complete control of my body's response. He wanted to show me that it needed him.

He kept me on the edge for so long my muscles were trembling. Sweat dripped down my back and thighs. Still he kept me pinned.

My body was completely tense. I held my breath. Liam paused. Then as his fingers pressed hard onto my aching, swollen clit, he bit down on my ass, just enough to excite and intensify the building waves of pleasure. Finally, the explosion came and I slammed my hips down, rubbing myself against his hand over and over as I screamed out his name.

He kept his hand on my center until the pulsing stopped. Then he slowly pulled it away. He kissed me all down my back and across both cheeks of my ass.

He leaned over to whisper in my ear. "Have a great holiday, sweetheart. I'll see you when you get back."

I was too spent to even say good-bye.

I fell into a blissful sleep on the deck chair, and had great dreams. They most likely involved Liam, because I woke up smiling. I wasn't sure how I was going to wean my body off its Liam addiction, but I would figure it out somehow. I let myself have that one final day to luxuriate in the physical wonder that was sex with that man.

Eventually I got a little stiff on the chair, and opted to resume my nap in bed. I opened my restocked fridge, grabbed a giant bottle of fresh-squeezed organic juice and a turkey sandwich, and made my way into my bedroom.

I was naked and chilled away from the heat lamp, so I got back into my pajamas, and grabbed a book I had been given for Christmas and had never had time to read.

I snuggled into my down comforter, flipped the page, took a giant bite of sandwich and grinned. I was the happiest I had been in a long time, and I let myself just enjoy it. I stayed in bed all day. So there.

CHAPTER THIRTY-SEVEN

The next morning, I was gifted with another early morning wake-up call from the apartment buzzer. It was Liam again, so I buzzed him in. I was completely torn and pretty much a mess. I knew I needed to stay away from him, but damn he was making it hard.

Or maybe my father and Chloe were right. Maybe I was just a stupid young woman, preprogrammed for mistakes and disasters. My head was a cloudy storm. It seemed whatever choice I made, I was somehow being foolish, or cowardly.

Still, he had been kind and understanding once, and, as he said, I owed it to him to listen.

I was surprised by his, well, rugged appearance. I suppose I had been expecting him to pull out all the stops in the attractiveness department, since he seemed to want to lure me back to our fun-and-pleasure-only agreement.

Instead, he had a little stubble and quite a lot of bedhead going on. Seeing as how the universe was conniving against me, though, he did of course still look wildly sexy. Why was I not just jumping into his arms again?

Oh, right. Because he had broken my heart, a heart that I had told him was fragile and just coming back to life. He had taken it gently in his sexy hands and smashed it onto the ground. Then he had stomped on it a few times for good measure. Everyone says to look at history to predict the future. So he would do it again. Anyone would tell me that.

INVITATION

I let him in to my apartment, and offered him some of the food he had brought over the day before.

He rubbed his hands together. "Is there any left?"

It made me laugh. "I can tell you've lived with guys. I ate all day yesterday and there is still a ton of food in there."

"Good." He moved toward the kitchen. "I've just gone online to learn how to make an omelet. It's going to knock your socks off."

"Don't count on it, Romeo." The previous morning's activities had been the relationship's finale. Best not to let him think it was any sort of beginning. "I'll get dressed."

"Wear stretchy stuff." What the hell? I peeked back around the corner, confusion written on my face.

"We're going rock climbing!" He put his arms in the air as though cheering. "Well, wall climbing, actually. But we'll pretend we're on some treacherous mountain." Again I laughed, but it was maybe more of a this-guy-has-lost-his-mind nervous sort of laugh.

"Okay, I'll play. Why?"

He moved through the kitchen, whipping eggs, hunting for pans. "Because my original plan was to come over here to tell you all about how my parents' horrific relationship, and my seriously disturbed childhood made me want to run away as soon as I realized I was falling in love with you..." He refused to make eye contact with me, and was busy melting butter into a skillet.

"What..." I started, but he held a hand up.

"But then I realized two things. One, I just don't want to talk about all that crap – even though I'm realizing that my tough guy routine might not be my best play anymore."

I couldn't help it. I laughed at the sight of this tough guy making an omelet for me. He always got me with the laughter.

He pretended to shoot me a disapproving look.

"And two...?" I encouraged.

"And two, the problem isn't my supposedly unresolved issues. The problem is that I acted like an asshole, right?"

Usually I would get all flustered and smother the other person with denials and encouragement, but this time I just nodded. "Yes. You did."

"So, the problem is that I hurt you when you needed someone the most." He slid the omelet onto a plate and put it on the table for me. He got me a knife and fork and a glass of juice.

I didn't answer the last question, because a painful lump had formed in my throat and my eyes were prickling with tears. He came to sit beside me.

"We can talk all day, but it won't make you trust me. It won't make your heart want me the way your body does." He couldn't help himself and smiled a little. He rubbed his hand against his face, trying to get rid of the possibly inappropriate grin.

"So, enough with the talking. I'm going to get you to trust me. In the next twenty four hours."

"By rock climbing?"

"It's a start. You'll see. It's sort of completely terrifying and exhilarating all at once. Remember you felt that way about sex at first, and then our bodies worked it out?"

"Yes. I remember that, vaguely." I rubbed at my throat to get rid of the lump, and tried to drink a little juice. I just picked at the omelet.

"So, now, I've got to get your heart to feel the same way about me: that being terrified is worth it." His shoulders slumped, discouraged. "I'm not saying this right."

"I think I understand. I'm not sure it can happen, though."

"I know."

"And what's with the twenty-four hours?"

He looked longingly at the omelet, so I slid it over to him. "Well, this is not ideal, obviously, but my advisor heard about an opening at a fellowship in New York. It would mean skipping ahead a little and basically working double shifts for who knows how long. But it's one of those once-in-a-lifetime things. The chance won't come along again."

"So, why's it a tough decision. You're not afraid of hard work. Once in a lifetime is once in a lifetime. Case closed."

He finished the omelet. He stood to clear the table. Then he came back to the table and stood behind me. He wrapped his arms around me, so that his mouth was against my neck. This was not a man who was prepared to fight fair.

"Case NOT closed, councilor. Because I currently have two once-in-a-lifetime chances in front me."

I wanted to turn to look at him, but didn't want my lips to end up right beside his. Also, there were some tears involved (for me). I wiped them away almost angrily.

"That's ridiculous,' I snapped. "Why would you give up a sure-thing amazing opportunity, for a maybe-we'll-go-on-some-more-dates sort of thing? Who would do that?"

"No one." He kissed the side of my head and then moved to the other side of my small table. He put his arms on the table, palms up, signaling he wanted to hold my hand. God help me, I couldn't resist. An electrical force came off this man and I wanted to have its warmth and power for myself. "I'm not giving up the fellowship for the possibility of another date. You are it for me."

"I don't understand."

"If we stay together, if I stay here, we'll make it. I know it."

"You can't know that."

"Yes, I can. I knew it before, that's why I ran. I'm twenty-seven, and I thought that was way too young to have found 'The One'."

"It is."

"No, it's not. What I realized was how hard it was waiting for twenty-seven years to find you, and how I don't want to make it through any more unless you're with me." He looked up at me then. He squeezed my hands a little too tightly. He looked sexy, of course, but afraid, stressed out. "I put myself in the future and saw that if I didn't put this out there, if I didn't risk it all to have you love me, I'd never forgive myself. I'd never get over you."

It was the most beautiful thing I'd ever heard. I wanted to leap over all my walls and fling myself at him. But my walls were strong and high.

"I can't take that kind of pressure. I would have to be worth giving up your career for. And I have 24 hours to decide? That's insane."

"It's not my career. I'm still going to have a good career. My father has the perfect career and is the saddest person I know. At least I figured that part out before becoming a bitter middle-aged alcoholic with the perfect career and the empty life."

I wanted to get all swept up in the moment. It seemed like the right thing to do, but we are who we are. "It feels like you're asking me to make that choice for you. I can't do it."

"No, I've made my choice. You're just in charge of yours." He stood. "Now, get dressed. I've got 22 hours left, and we're late for that climbing wall."

CHAPTER THIRTY-EIGHT

Climbing up a vertical wall, voluntarily, is an interesting experience.

We made good time with the traffic and weren't late after all. When we arrived, everyone shouted "Liam!", like in that old show 'Cheers' where everyone shouts "Norm!" whenever he walks it. It was clear he had been here once or twice before.

Liam walked over to the equipment desk. He had a duffel bag full of his own stuff, but we needed to rent some for me.

You have to wear a harness while wall climbing. It is not an elegant thing, but it is useful. I felt like a frumpy old fool in some sort of ancient chastity belt, and I wished I could joke with Liam about it. But I thought it would seem like flirting, which wasn't fair. It would be too misleading. I was back to never knowing what we were and were not allowed to do in our relationship.

Liam was right. It was going to be all or nothing with us. Our feelings had never really been casual at all. I had used that as an excuse, to allow myself to test the waters and to reenter the whole "physical" world slowly and with control. Liam had used the excuse to keep himself from any suffocating commitments, and a life like his parents'. When he had kissed me on that final day and said, "I think we're in trouble," he had been absolutely right. Now we had to decide whether to run from that trouble, or to embrace all the risks.

I am not good at embracing risks.

Liam, damn him, somehow managed to retain his dignity and sex appeal in the ridiculous climbing gear. He shifted things around a little so that the harness didn't exaggerate his package too much, but there wasn't much he could do. I suspect that being displayed that way might be one of the reasons men like this climbing business. It is the only possible explanation for the hideousness of cycling shorts, but I'll leave that rant for another day.

Thankfully, Liam offered to go first. Since I had no idea what was happening, this seemed like a reasonable plan. I figured I would walk over to the water cooler and hang out for an hour or so, but no, I was to be immediately involved. I had to hold on to his rope!

"Think of it as a trust exercise," he smiled.

"I can't hold you up. I'm not that strong."

"Yes you are. But it doesn't matter anyway. I hold myself up. This is just for if I fall."

"Super . . ."

"If I fall," he continued. "The lever will take most of my weight. You just keep your hands on the rope, and your eyes on me. You'll be fine." He gave me a quick kiss on the side of my face. I appreciated that he was being warm towards me, but not too presumptuous.

"And try not to stare at my ass." He joked. "I know how you ladies can be." He walked toward the wall, reached over his head to grab a fake-rock-thing and started climbing.

I tried not to admire the physicality of him, but I didn't stand much of a chance. First because that was my job, and his life was in my hands. It was required of me to watch his every move. I actually couldn't turn away.

Secondly, because, I swear, he was like a living god. I had seen him naked, so it's not like there was a part of him that was a surprise. But I had never really seen him in motion. He had both strength and grace. His legs were lean and muscular. His back muscles rippled under his shirt. I found myself staring at his long fingers, grabbing onto the rocks and pulling him up with tremendous power. I marveled at how gentle those fingers had been on my body.

I was equal parts completely turned on, and completely frustrated with myself. Is that all I was? Just a friggin' lust machine? It seemed like a mature reasonable person ought to be able to think with more than her tingling parts, and I was determined to be that person. The stronger my lust grew, the more I hardened my heart to him.

Eventually, Liam made it to the top. He didn't do any silly victory-whatever someone does when they're at the top of a rock and hanging by a thread. He just slapped the top and started making his way back down. I saw other climbers repelling down quickly, but Liam was having fun climbing. He took another way down, and really pushed his body. Not that I noticed.

When he was back on the ground, he came toward me, sweaty and happy. He wanted to kiss me, and I wished it could all be so simple and sweet. But it wasn't. I turned my head away and moved to the wall.

"Not too scared?"

"Yes, I am too scared. But I'll do it."

"That's my girl."

"I'm not. I'm not your girl. Please stop saying things like that."

"Why?"

"Because it makes me feel sad, and stressed out. I promised I'd spend this day with you, and I'm going to. But when you say things like that, I feel like I'm leading you on or something."

"I don't think that."

"But this isn't going to change anything. I love that you thought up all this stuff, and that you understand why I don't trust you..."

"But . . ."

"But, I don't. I don't trust you. Not really. I know you won't let me fall to my death here. But there are other ways to fall."

Liam stopped working the rope through my harness and looked at me. Really looked at me. His face had been playful, then earnest, but as I said this, his face turned angry.

He dropped the rope to the ground and strode off to the change benches.

"Liam! Let's do this. I promised I would, and I will."

He spun towards me, and the look on his face made me take a step back. "Don't do me any favors, Madison. Give me a break! The only reason you're here is because you owe me?"

His anger was unnerving, but I couldn't back down. "Yes. You reminded me that you had listened to me and been supportive of me. So, I'm doing the same. I'm trying to listen. I'm trying to be supportive."

He turned away from me, struggling to get out of his gear. I stood by, watching helplessly.

"You know Madison, the first time I met you I knew you were the most beautiful woman I had ever seen. The first time I talked to you, I thought you were the bravest and smartest, too." He balled up his clothes, shoving them into his duffel bag. "But you're not brave. You're a coward who doesn't want to try something amazing because she might get hurt. And you're not smart, or you'd realize what a lame-ass excuse that is. I made one mistake. One goddamn mistake. We are amazing together. Amazing!" He turned away from me, trying to catch his breath. I was glad, because I thought I might cry, and I didn't want him to see it.

He spoke very quietly. "I deserved another chance." He walked to the door. "So screw you, Madison. You're free. I'm done."

CHAPTER THIRTY-NINE

I got changed, and then sat on the bench wondering what to do. All I had brought with me was my driver's license for ID and my Visa, which was useless, since it was almost certainly maxed.

I was feeling overwhelmed and emotional. Was I angry, hurt, sad? Who even knew anymore? It was all a mess. I needed to focus on the problem in front of me, though. It was like a riddle to be solved.

Who to call for help? It was hard to accept that there really wasn't anyone I could call. I had lots of acquaintances at school and the hospital, but could I call one of them on a Sunday morning? And ask them to drive way the hell out here to warehouse-zone Seattle? There was that guy who seemed really into me when I went out to dinner with the other interns, but I wasn't interested in him. And I wasn't the kind of person who could take advantage of someone else that way.

Chloe? Ha. Parents? Ha. I was trying to think if I had any cash lying around at home. Maybe a cab could take me home, and then wait while I ran in. Doubtful. Plus, this was going to be a fifty-dollar cab ride at least.

I was on the verge of panic, but I thought I'd give my subconscious a chance to mull it over. I closed my eyes and leaned back against the wall. I was trying to breath, live in the moment, all that stuff. It was working a little. I was, at the very least, feeling how completely exhausting my current life had become. One way or another, I was going to have to make some big changes.

Once more, the air moved across my face and I knew Liam had come back in. I kept my eyes closed, but sensed him coming. He stopped in front of me.

"I'm sorry," we both started. I opened my eyes to find him looking down at me. He wasn't smiling, but he also wasn't angry anymore. He just seemed sad. Beaten.

"I remembered you didn't bring your purse. I'm pissed, but not enough to leave you stranded out here." He put out his hand and I took it. He lifted me to standing and we stood face to face.

"I got so angry because you mean a lot to me. I don't know how to make this better."

"Neither do I."

"Okay." He sighed, resigned. "You ready?" He kept hold of my hand and pulled me to the door. He waved sadly at his gang of climbing buddies as we left. I didn't make eye contact with any of them. They were probably glaring at me.

We got into his car. Just as we were settling in, my phone started ringing.

"Oh, it's the hospital," I said.

"Don't answer it!" Liam exclaimed. "That Emerg's number. They're probably short-staffed and calling you in."

"Then I need to answer!" He tried to pry the phone from my fingers, but I swiveled away.

"Hello."

"Is this Madison Spencer?" a gruff male voice asked. Behind him I could hear the beepings and general chaos of the Emergency room. Liam had been right.

"Yes, it is."

"Tell them you don't start until tomorrow," Liam interjected. I pushed him away. I couldn't get off to such a bad start. That would show a great attitude. But this was also the only weekend I'd had off in over two months.

"I'm starting my rotation tomorrow," I offered, hoping against odds that the person would say, "Oh, well, in that cause, enjoy the afternoon, dear!"

Instead he said, "Do you know Alexander Mathis?" It took a second to recognize the name. Alex. Mario Andretti.

"Sure, I know Alex." I looked to Liam, who was looking as confused and concerned I was.

"Well, he's been brought in, and he says you're his doctor."

"That's flattering, but I'm just an intern."

"Doesn't matter to me, and I don't have time for a debate about it. He's sick. He'd like to see you. What you do about it is your own concern." He hung up. Guess I was going to have to get used to a different type of personality down there.

I turned to Liam. "Nice fellow."

He smiled. "It was McAllister. I could hear him loud and clear."

"I bet. Anyway, Alex is back in Emergency. He wants to see me." I fiddled with the phone. "Is that inappropriate or something? Some kind of patient-doctor boundary thing?"

Liam turned away from me and started the car. "Jesus, Madison. You analyze the life out of everything. He's a little kid who's probably scared and you're the name he remembers. Are we going in or what?"

I liked that he said 'we'. I did want to see Alex. But I was afraid of what I'd find.

CHAPTER FORTY

We made good time to the hospital. Nice weather and Sunday morning combined to keep traffic reasonable. We parked on the street a block away, and hurried into the Emergency department.

This time it was a group of nurses who waved and yelled, "Hey, Liam." This was one popular man.

One of the nurses, an attractive blonde, came toward us and looked me over. There was nothing I could do but stand there. I was in yoga pants and a t-shirt. My hair had barely been combed that morning. I let her have her fill. She turned back to Liam, "You here with us now?"

"No," he answered. "McAllister called Dr. Spencer." He gestured to me. "A patient is asking for her."

"Oh!" The nurse's features softened, and she patted my arm. "Alex told me he wanted to see you." She turned to Liam. "You were his second choice, but he really wanted Madison."

"Don't we all," replied Liam grimly.

The nurse shot him a perplexed look, but quickly turned back to me.

"Where is he?"

She took my hand and I felt a cold shiver pass through me. She pulled me over to the nursing station and sat me down in a chair.

"He's septic. He was just in here last week with pneumonia."

I nodded. "Yes, I saw him."

"So you saw how thin and pale he was then?"

Yes, I had. But he was a little kid with leukemia. Of course he was pale and thin. "But he was on antibiotics. He was fighting it really well."

"He's still fighting," she said, and relief flooded my body. "But he might not win this one."

I wanted to slap her. Who was she to be so negative?

"Where is he?" I stood up and began looking at the charts along the desk, checking for his name.

"He's in Peds ICU. The infection's in his blood now. The antibiotics can only really work if his immune system is helping, and his can't. There's nothing left."

"Don't say that." I sounded like a child, but the nurse was kind.

"His system is shutting down. Nothing's for certain, but his kidneys are failing."

"Is he unconscious?" Liam asked.

"In and out."

I pictured this delirious, terrified child. My body started to shake. In an attempt to disguise my nerves and weakness I stood and started walking toward the main hospital. "I'm going up," I told them.

"Wait for me," said Liam.

We rode the elevator in silence. I was afraid I would start crying. It would be hugely unprofessional. I was supposed to be able to put on a strong 'doctorly' face, right? How long until I actually got the hang of it?

I was more worried about frightening Alex. He would see my face and know exactly how bad things were. That's another perk of being a hospital kid. They're even better than their parents at figuring out what's going on.

We made it into PICU and quickly moved toward Alex's bed. His parents were with him. They stood as we approached, and Mrs. Mathis reached out to embrace me. "Thank you so much for coming. He's just crazy about both of you." I held her tightly. At that moment, professionalism could go screw itself. Mr. Mathis stood and took her back into his arms.

I went to stand beside Alex's bed. He looked smaller than ever. I stroked what was left of his shiny golden hair. The chemo had stolen it from him, but his face was still covered in those happy freckles.

"We think he'll make it," Mr. Mathis said. Mrs. Mathis nodded eagerly. "He's a fighter. He's been fighting most of his life, and he'll make it through this, too." They looked so certain; their optimism was contagious. I started to believe it, too.

"Do you mind if I stay a bit?" I asked them. I looked down at my clothing. "I'm so sorry I look like this. I would never normally come to see him looking this way . . ."

"Don't even think about it. You came running in on your day off. We love you for it." Mrs. Mathis looked at Liam, too. "Both of you." She smiled, remembering something. "Alex wants you to get married. Did you know that?"

Liam said, "Yes" at the exact moment I said "No."

I wanted to change the subject. "I'll talk to Alex about that when he wakes up." I didn't know if he was sleeping or unconscious and I couldn't ask at that point. I didn't want to make his parents even more upset.

Liam sat in an extra chair. He was comfortable with these people. He cared about Alex, too. "Why don't you two go have a bite to eat?" They shook their heads, no, but without much conviction. They had probably been up since midnight.

"I don't think I could eat, but I could use a glass of water. And a bathroom break." Mr. Mathis stood. "Come on, honey. He's in good hands." He looked at us both and smiled sadly. "Just page us if you need us."

They walked slowly into the hallway, holding each other up. They were wonderful people, a wonderful loving couple. We both watched them, but didn't say anything to each other.

I pulled a chair closer to the bed so I could hold Alex's hand. "Is he in a coma?" I asked Liam.

"I think so. I haven't seen his chart. But this doesn't look like sleep to me."

I put Alex's hand to my cheek. "But his parents are right. Kids get sick so fast, but sometimes they get well so fast, too. He's a tough little guy."

I smiled and started to relax a bit.

Suddenly, though, a shrill and prolonged beep came from the machine above Alex's head.

"Oh, he's coding." Liam leapt to his feet and ran to the nursing station. They were already on the phone calling a Code Blue. Liam grabbed the crash cart and pushed it into the room.

"Madison, you have to move."

I got out of the way. "Let me help. Please!"

But I was just in the way. Two more residents appeared in an instant, and then the respiratory techs. There were more than enough bodies. Liam turned to me, "Go find his parents."

It was the last thing in the world I wanted to do in that minute, but my legs carried me along. I didn't get far. Mr. and Mrs. Mathis were already racing back to the unit. They had heard the alarm and feared the worst.

When they saw me running, they knew it was Alex. Fear clutched at them. They ran right past me, and tried to get in his room.

Liam tried to intercept them, but they pushed past him. On the bed, the medical staff were performing CPR in between shocks. It was a sight no parent should ever witness. I grabbed them both and pulled them to me. "Don't watch. They're doing everything. Alex knows you're here, I promise."

We stood together outside of the room, getting the occasional glimpse of Alex through the glass partition. Liam stood to one side, letting the cardiology residents and the respiratory people do their jobs. We both wanted to jump in and help, but we knew it was better for us to just stay out of the way.

Liam looked stoic, but shaken. He turned away. I met his eyes with mine and we just looked at one another as the chaos boiled around us.

Then we all heard it: one short beep, and then another. His heart was working again, the rhythm quickly stabilizing. It was weak but steady. Alex' parents rushed to his side. We all watched for twenty minutes, making sure he was really back with us.

The hospital staff packed up the equipment and supplies, smiling and chatting. They picked up the discarded wrapping from the tubes and IV's.

It was a huge reprieve. He hadn't died. Liam came up behind me. "You need to sit down." I tried to argue, but felt my knees give out. It had been a tough few days. I hadn't eaten much. How did this man know my body better than it knew itself? "I want to get you home."

"It's okay." It wasn't fair to take advantage of his kind nature.

"You can get rid of me tomorrow. Tonight, I'm taking care of you."

CHAPTER FORTY-ONE

I don't remember the walk home. I kept seeing Alex's little body being jolted, and his parents sobbing. Images of Isabel in Owen's bed kept popping up, too, and I could hardly believe it had been less than seventy-two hours since it happened. Liam had come back, and now I was losing him again. It was so much to deal with.

Liam and I held hands. It was all the communication we needed. The morning would separate us, but for now we had company and comfort and we both knew to take whatever was offered. Life was short. Caring people, rare.

Once we were at my apartment, Liam turned to me. "I don't know if I should stay. I want to make sure you're okay, but I know you probably want me to go."

I couldn't bear to watch him walk away. Not yet. "Don't leave." I pulled him toward the door that I held open.

When we got to my apartment, we were moving like ghosts. There was no way to assimilate it all. I offered to make tea, and Liam accepted. We stood together in the kitchen waiting for the water to boil. We got mugs and tea bags. When the water was ready, we poured it.

By this point, an ominous shaking had started deep inside me. I felt like there was an earthquake starting in the middle of my abdomen. I felt the blood draining out of my face and my hands trembling. I tried to say something to Liam, but my jaw was shaking and my throat was so tight I couldn't form any words.

I tried to lift my cup but my hand shook so badly, I spilled the boiling tea all over it. Liam grabbed my hand and pushed it under cold water from the tap. He looked closely at me then.

"Oh, sweetheart, you're so pale. I think you're in shock. You have to lie down." He scooped me up and carried me into my bedroom. He sat me on the bed, plumping pillows up behind me. "You need sugar." He ran back to the kitchen to get juice and cookies and brought them back.

"I can't," I choked out.

"Drink." He put the cup to my lips. He left the room and came back with bandages and antibiotic ointment. He smoothed it onto my burned hand with exquisite tenderness, and then wrapped the gauze around it, tucking in the last little bit. "I don't have tape with me," he explained.

His kindness was the last straw, and tears streamed down my face. I wiped them away frantically, afraid that I would start sobbing in that scary, can't catch my breath way I do when I am virtually hysterical.

Liam held my hands off my face and waited until I looked into his eyes. He leaned forward and kissed each cheek. Then he pulled back slightly. He moved forward again and touched my lips gently with his. I couldn't respond, but I didn't move away.

He leaned forward and kissed me again. I started to shake. I was so cold. I have never been so cold. My teeth were chattering and my body shook.

Liam grabbed extra blankets from the cupboard and wrapped them around me, but nothing helped.

He climbed into the bed and held me until I stopped shivering. He stroked my hair and kissed my cheek, my ear, and my neck. I felt full of sadness and despair, and I needed his warmth and his light.

"I need to feel your skin," I said. He sat up and took off everything but his underwear. Then he sat me up and undressed me, too.

INVITATION

We lay down. Our bodies felt awkward at first, but they soon wrapped around each other perfectly. He smelled like life and goodness. I needed to breathe him in.

Every inch of my skin ached to touch him. I ran my hands along his back. I pressed my cheek against his and breathed in the smell of him. I buried my face in his beautiful hair. I wanted to be connected to him. I wanted to melt into him, to merge with his goodness.

He kissed me again, and my lips kissed back. We stayed wrapped around each other, kissing and caressing. It felt like hours passed. It was a gentle, slow-burning passion. There was less urgency, because our bodies knew it would work, and knew it would be perfect.

He rolled me onto my stomach and began kissing my neck and back. He ran his hands, light as feathers across my skin until I shivered with pleasure and comfort.

He rolled me onto my back and kissed my face again and again. He moved to lie between my legs. I stared up into his eyes and saw such kindness.

"Is this okay?" he whispered.

"Yes." I needed him more at that moment than I ever had. It wasn't a sexual need. It was a need to reassert life, to push back misery even just for a minute, to forget our troubled complex lives and embrace this simple moment, this simple bliss.

I moved to push my panties down. He looked at me with such intensity. I pushed his underwear down, too. I need to wrap myself around him. I needed to be connected to something meaningful and good. I didn't want us to be separate people. Alone we were so small and frail. I wanted him to be a part of me.

He entered me slowly and paused to kiss me more. We stayed that way for a long time. I wrapped my legs around his waist to draw him deeper into me. The pleasures were soft and sweet.

We started moving together as though we were floating on waves. It was effortless and perfect. It was joyful and healing.

We kept it very slow. We were in no hurry. We wanted it to last. Either it was a new beginning or a last goodbye. Neither of us knew yet, but either way it was important.

Slowly, our bodies began to move with greater urgency. The rhythm remained smooth, but the waves we were riding grew larger. Soon we were gripped by that innate rhythm that presses bodies together perfectly. We collided with greater force, but stayed wrapped together, kissing passionately.

Only in the last moments did our mouths separate, each to cry out in release and joy. The joy of coming back to life.

CHAPTER FORTY-TWO

Just before dawn, I heard Liam getting out of bed. I kept my eyes closed and enjoyed the warm bed and the peace inside of me. I felt safe and cared for. We had definitely gone beyond just lust.

How could I have ever felt that the sex with Liam was just sex? It had always been something special, even when we were trying so hard to convince ourselves it wasn't.

The night before was on a different level. It wasn't the sheet clenching, shoulder biting pheromone-fest we had created together before; it was soft and slow and sweet. It felt like our bodies were talking to each other. They had known all along that they belonged together, and they had finally convinced our hearts to join in as well.

I heard Liam rustling around and figured he was scavenging for food. The man was always hungry, and we'd had almost nothing to eat yesterday. I heard him come back into my room and sit in my comfortable armchair.

I heard pages turning and a pencil scribbling. I figured he was preparing for his day. This was the day he was supposed to tell his advisor if he was going to New York. If I told him I wanted him to stay, would he really do it? My heart lurched at the thought of opening up to him again only for him to change his mind and crush me. What if it was just the thrill of the chase for him? Lots of my friends have had guys desperate for them until they agreed to go out with them. Then the interest suddenly waned, and just as the girl was really falling for the guy, he ditched her; then she spent more time healing a broken heart than they had spent together as a couple.

But was that Liam? How could I ever know? I thought back to the wondrous physical moments we had shared before he started ignoring me. It had never been just about the fun and the passion. Chloe had been right about that. But she had been wrong about the true feelings. They had been there, all right, in every sweet kiss, in every nibbled lip and caressed breast. Each gasp and moan had been for pleasure, but also for joy, the joy of finding someone wildly exciting as well as grown-up and kind. It was a sort of miracle to find a person like that at all. And to find a person who felt the same way I did? That was like winning the lottery.

But what if he hurt me again? What if? I thought of all the moments since he had deserted me. I thought of how hard I had worked at the hospital, about the terrible times with Owen. I thought about helping Isabel, and getting a great review from Olsen the Ogre. I realized that Liam had hurt me, and it had taken me down for a few days. But I had survived. I was stronger than I knew. If he hurt me again, I would live.

I was crazy about him. I wanted to try to build something with him. Maybe he was going to be The One. I hoped so, but if he wasn't, I would be all right. For the first time, I realized that our experiment had worked. I had been brought back to life: not just my body, but also my heart, my courage, my passion for life. All of it.

I was never going to let anyone take that away from me again, even Liam. And because I now knew that, I could let him in. The risks suddenly seemed so small, the potential so huge.

Of course I would ask him to stay.

I pushed the blanket off me, trying to will myself to get up, but I was so comfortable, so relaxed. I drifted back into my happy almost asleep state. I started hearing a funny swoosh-click sound. I thought I had imagined it, or was halfway into a dream.

But it came again and again. And then I suddenly realized what it was.

I sat up, my eyes wide open, and saw Liam standing over me with his phone in his hands. He was taking pictures.

"What are you doing?" I screamed. I went from happily half-asleep to half-insane in a split second. There was nothing rational about me at that point. Some internal sense of terror and survival rushed back, taking over all my senses, my body and my mind.

I was back in that disgusting bathroom, covered in beer and piss. Filthy words were written on me and people laughed. The cameras clicked and clicked, but I couldn't get up. Someone stuck his finger in me, and they all laughed again and took more pictures.

Later, when I had been to the emergency, and gone through the brutal exam needed to collect samples for a rape kit, after I had showered a hundred times in almost boiling water, after the cruel words written in permanent marker had finally started to fade, after all that, the pictures started showing up online.

And then it just got worse and worse.

I couldn't seem to snap back into the present. My body and mind were in both places at once. I grabbed my robe and struggled to put it on. I felt like I was being attacked. Liam was talking, and moving toward me, but I slapped the phone out of his hand and pushed him backwards, hard.

I ran to pick the phone up off the floor and started scrolling. I saw picture after picture of me lying on the bed, naked.

"What is this? How could you do this?"

Liam tried to interrupt, but the words just flew from me. "What the hell is wrong with you? Why are you all such fucking pigs?" I erased picture after picture and started sobbing. "How could I fall for this? How could I have believed this would be different?"

Liam moved to hold my arm, but I struck out, batting him away. I curled into myself, the sobs rattling me. "I'm such an idiot."

Liam crept closer. "Maddie, it's not what you think." I didn't even respond. What was there to say? How could he explain away taking naked pictures while I slept?

"I'm so, so sorry. I wasn't thinking. Here, I need to show you something." He stood up and brought a sketchpad over to me. I wouldn't look at it. He laid it on the ground beside me.

"I draw pictures. I always have. Lately they've all been of you." He was flipping through the book, pushing pictures at me. I closed my eyes.

"I was afraid that this morning was going to be it for us. You were there in the bed looking more beautiful than I've ever seen you look, with this sweet little smile on your face." He sat down, trying to catch his breath. He was panting, trying to talk quickly before I shut him down.

"I couldn't draw it fast enough. I needed a picture, to remind me. So I could finish my sketch later. I wanted something to remember you by."

I kept silent, making sure he was finished. It was creative. He was fast on his feet, and quick with a clever lie. I'll give him that.

"Get out of my house."

"Oh, Maddie. Don't end it like this."

I said it again, calmly and coldly. "Get away from me. Get out of here." I stayed curled up, knees under my chin, arms around my legs. I didn't move at all.

Liam seemed to be trying to say more. He kept opening his mouth and closing it. I couldn't wait for him to shut up and leave me alone. Finally, he stood and walked out.

I put my head down on my knees, ready to cry again; but nothing came out. I was too tired. There were no tears left.

CHAPTER FORTY-THREE

I climbed back into bed. It smelled like Liam, which made me feel sick, so I got up. I showered. I forced myself to eat some cereal.

I had another new rotation starting that day.

I envy all those great characters in books and on TV who get to just fall apart and stay in their apartments eating too much and watching sad movies. I wonder if there really are people like that in real life.

The people I know have to go to work. There is a schedule, and if I don't show up, someone else does a double shift. Someone else works forty-eight hours straight.

If I messed up, the people I worked with would pay for it; and then I'd get a bad grade for being unreliable. There's no room for weakness, not physical illness, and certainly not a broken heart.

I went into my bedroom and stripped the sheets off the bed. If I were rich, I would have thrown them away. I would have thrown the whole bed away if I could.

I got dressed and did my hair. I packed up my things.

I moved to the window to crack it open a little. The room was full of pain and ghosts; it needed airing out. My toe hit something on the floor and I looked down to see Liam's sketchpad.

It was like it glowed with radioactive menace. I knew not to touch it, but it was nearly impossible to resist.

I picked up the book. I wanted to walk straight out to the dumpster and throw it in. Of course I didn't do that. I sat on the edge of the bed and opened to the front page.

It was a drawing of a young boy and girl. They were on the swings, heads tilted back, mouths open in wide smiles. They seemed almost alive.

Liam was so good at this. There was so much about him that I didn't know.

I kept flipping. There were wonderful portraits of faces. I didn't know any of them, until I flipped to a page with Alex on it. He was burning down the hallway in his wheelchair. I smiled, remembering our meeting on my first day of work.

I dreaded seeing the pictures closer to the back of the sketchbook. I was sure there would be no pictures of me at all, proving that Liam was a liar. Or worse, there would be something vile and disgusting.

I turned the page and froze. Liam had drawn a picture of us on the bridge. It was from behind, how he must have imagined we looked. I could see our bodies leaning into one another, trying to be closer but keeping it safe. It was shaded dark, and the lights sparkled around the couple in the picture. Us. He had captured exactly how I had felt that night.

The next picture was of my face on a pillow. I was asleep. The entire picture spoke of 'peace'.

The next drawing was a profile of my face. My head was thrown back, eyes closed, mouth open. Hair cascaded down my back. Pleasure was in every line.

I couldn't bear to look at all of them. I flipped to the last drawing.

It was of me, again. This morning. I was on my side, blanket removed. I was naked, but it was discreet. My right arm covered most of my breasts. I was tilted slightly forward, so my right leg covered my pelvis.

It was a beautiful picture. Beams of sunlight peeked through the shades. Every curve of the sheets, of my body, was sensual. And something else. There was something in the picture that I couldn't identify. Some feeling it evoked. It was sexy in a way, but it was more than that, too.

I ran my fingers down the lines of the body in the picture and pretended I was Liam, watching me sleeping in the bed, and then copying me here, on the page.

I suddenly knew exactly what the picture was saying.

CHAPTER FORTY-FOUR

I scrambled to gather the rest of my things together, and shoved my arms into my coat. I was running down the hallway before my shoes were even completely on.

I wanted to run all the way to the hospital, but got stopped at the first set of lights. It gave me a chance to text Liam. All I could say was 'write back a.s.a.p.' and then it was time to run again. All the way to the hospital I kept trying to text and call. He didn't answer.

What if I was too late? What if he had already told his advisor he would go? What if he had just slammed the door on us, tired of the drama and wanting to just get on with his own life? That's what I had done when things got tough.

I got to the hospital and tried to decide which way to go first. Alex! Of course he would see how Alex was doing. I ran for the elevators and pushed the floor for PICU. I stopped running, it seemed disrespectful, but I walked really quickly into Alex's room. No Liam.

"Hello, dear," said Mrs. Mathis. I smiled at her at looked over at Alex. His eyes were open, those gorgeous eyelashes framing the greenest of eyes.

"Hi you!" I moved over to his bed. "I really want to talk to you, but I have to do some things first." He nodded. "And, uh, by the way, have you seen Liam. Dr. Mason?"

"Yes, we have," piped in Mrs. Mathis. "He looked dreadful. Is he ill?"

I didn't know how to answer that, and time was short. "I'll be back later. I've really got to go." As I raced away, I looked down at my phone.

Would he have gone straight to his advisor's office from here? Before he had a chance to change his mind? I hoped not, but figured he probably would have. That's what I would have done; committed myself to something I couldn't get out of, to force myself into a decision I didn't really want to make.

I wasn't exactly sure where his advisor's office was. I tried to remember his name. Liam had mentioned it once in passing, but it had been a common name. Nothing about it really stood out.

I went to the administration wing and just started racing past the doors, looking at the names. I was red-faced and sweaty, and verging on desperate. I kept hoping Liam would have mercy on me and page me back, but there was only radio silence.

Maybe he couldn't respond? Maybe he was in a meeting with all the hospital bigwigs, who were right now patting him on the back and telling him how prestigious the opportunity was, how fortunate he was, and how much they'd miss him . . .

I passed door after door. Jesus, how many administrators did one hospital need? And then I heard him. I heard Liam's sexy low grumble. Which door? I pressed my ear to several until I found it. Campbell. Right! Dr. Campbell.

Before I could stop myself I banged on the door. Not a knock. A bang. The voices stopped. The door opened, and there stood Liam. He was still my beautiful man, but he did look ill. Ashen and beaten down.

I looked at Dr. Campbell. "Excuse me. I need him for a minute."

I started to pull Liam out as Dr. Campbell stood up. "Young lady! We're in the middle of something here."

"Oh, I'm aware of that." I pulled Liam all the way out and shut the door.

Liam stared down at me. "What the hell are you doing?" He put his hand on the doorknob, to go back in. I grabbed it and started pulling him down the hall. I found the door to the stairwell, and we went into it.

I was out of breath, trying to figure out what to say. I had been in such a hurry, I hadn't had time to organize my thoughts into anything another person could possibly understand.

I put my hands on his chest to steady myself and took some deep breaths. "I looked at the drawings." I looked into his eyes.

"Okay. Good, I guess." He looked away.

I put my hand against his cheek, turning him back to look at me. "No, I really looked at them. I saw what was there."

I wanted to tell him that I had seen what he had done. How every picture had captured not just the person he was drawing, but a feeling. I had seen joy and peace, bliss and longing, passion and . . . In all the drawings of me, in every curve, in the brightness of my eyes, in the contours of my body, I had seen love. Love.

But it was too hard to explain it all. I couldn't figure out how to say all these important things quickly enough. Liam was already turning away from me again. I grabbed the sides of his face and turned him to look at me. I was so terrified that my hands were trembling and I could hardly breathe. It was now or never. I looked into his beautiful, confused eyes and told him the simplest version of the truth: "I love you."

CHAPTER FORTY-FIVE

Liam stood completely still. For the first time ever, I could get no read on him. His feelings were hidden from me. He was going to tell me to go to hell, I knew it. But it was worth the chance. He was worth everything.

"Please don't go," I whispered.

He looked down at me, and then closed his eyes. It looked like he was in terrible pain. I braced myself to listen to whatever angry words were about to be flung at me.

But he didn't yell. My hands were still on his chest, and he took them in his own. He lifted them up to his neck, then wrapped his arms around my waist and pulled me up to him. I wrapped my legs around his middle and held on with all my might.

I started to kiss him, but we were laughing and talking and kissing all at once. He whispered in my ear, "I hope you meant that, because I am never going to let you go."

Liam pulled me by the hand, back down the hall to Dr. Campbell's office. He knocked and then peeked his head in the door. "Sorry, sir, I'm staying. You're stuck with me. Also, I really need today off. I'm not on call, the charting is done…"

I heard the gruff voice behind the door, "This is highly irregular, Dr. Mason…"

"Special situation, sir. I've really got to go." He closed the door gently and looked at me. We both tried to suppress our huge smiles. We were just two good kids cutting school for the first time ever.

"What about me?" I asked him. "I'm starting Emergency today."

"Don't worry about it. I'll talk to the nurses. They know we were up all night with Alex. They'll keep the doctors off your back."

"But, it'll look bad. I can't just skip out."

Liam stopped in his tracks. "Stop this. We are good, hard-working people. When did you last have a sick day?"

I was almost embarrassed to say it. "I've never had a sick day."

"Well, you're having one today. I'll write you a note." We both laughed again and made for the exit.

It was finally April and when I wasn't looking, Spring had happened. How had I not noticed? In the last day, the trees had bloomed and the happy chirping of birds was everywhere. It was a beautiful day. We walked together, holding hands, stopping to kiss at ridiculously frequent intervals.

"I want to go on a date with you." Liam said suddenly.

I smiled. "I think we're a little past that."

"Yeah, I know. We are in the exact right place, but there are some steps we missed somehow. I want to go on a real date."

"It's too damn cold still for a balloon ride..." I joked.

He smiled and pulled me into him again. "No, just something simple. I want to dress up. I want to eat something delicious. I want to go home with you and flirt and wonder if we're going to make it into bed."

He was right. It was so simple, but it sounded amazing. "I'd love that," I exclaimed, and meant it.

He looked down at his watch. "Okay, it's ten o'clock. I'll come and get you at noon."

I laughed. "Oh boy, a sexy lunch!" I enjoyed teasing him.

He wasn't smiling. "You have no idea how sexy a lunch can be." He kissed me hard and my mouth responded quickly. The feelings were immediate and intense. I began to doubt we were going to make it to lunch at all.

"And," he continued, "if the après-lunch flirting goes well, I want to have all afternoon so I can seduce you over and over again."

"Jesus, you've got to stop talking like that." I could barely stand. I was swooning, like one of those Victorian heroines.

"Less talk, more action?" He cupped my ass and pulled me into his erection. Then he gently pushed me away. "See, this is what I mean! I can't seem to keep my hands off you. No wonder you thought it was only about sex. I need to prove to you that it's much, much more." He looked so troubled and so sincere.

But all my doubts were gone. I was the one who had believed it was either lust or love. He had both for me, and the combination was perfection.

I pulled his face to mine and kissed it gently all over. I stopped at his lips and we kissed each other until we could hardly pull apart.

"There's nothing left to prove. I can see how much you care about me. I absolutely love you."

"I love you, too." Liam grabbed me, lifting me off the ground to kiss me.

"You don't have to say that now, just because I did. It's okay." I smiled up at him. It was okay. I could see we would get there, just as Liam had said we would.

"No, baby, I've loved you for a long time. For so long," and he started kissing me and clutching at me.

Once again, I could hardly talk. "I want to go home."

"Now," he said. "No lunch?"

"No, no lunch. Consider the flirtation a success. Take me home."

CHAPTER FORTY-SIX

It started raining, again, and we scrambled to get home. We slowed our pace once we were safely in the door. Liam took my coat off slowly, stopping to kiss me every few seconds. We were moving toward the bedroom, but Liam pulled me into the living room.

"I've never noticed this."

"The window?" I couldn't see what he meant.

"No, the way there's a step up to the window." I still wasn't getting it.

"Step up there," he said. I did.

I was facing him. He pulled me closer, and his hard-on pushed against my already swollen center. We both groaned. "Nice." I smiled.

"Turn around," he said, his voice husky with need once more. This time his erection was pushing against my ass. I pushed back into it, increasing the pressure and pleasure for both of us.

"Don't move. I want to undress you."

I stood with my back to him, trembling with anticipation as he removed each piece of clothing. He reached forward and undid the buttons of my blouse, brushing against my breasts each time. It dropped to the floor in a silky rustle.

He undid my bra and slid it off my shoulders, down my arms. He ran his fingers lightly along the insides of my arms as he made his way back up to my breasts.

He pushed his hand down the waistband of my pants and under the elastic of my panties. His fingers spread the lips of my cleft open and touched the tender wet flesh between. I inhaled sharply, still amazed at how incredible that first touch always was.

He groaned and pulled me back against his erection. "I love that you get so wet for me." His fingers explored, while I writhed in pleasure. He pinched me gently between his fingers, and rubbed me until I was breathing hard.

He took his hand from my pants and undid the button and zipper. He shimmied my clothing down past my hips, and I stepped out of them. I turned to hold him.

Because of the rise in the floor, our pelvises were together and our mouths were almost at the same height. I wrapped my arms more tightly around him, enjoying the curves of his muscles, the feeling of barely controlled power under his skin.

He kissed me, and then stopped. "Turn around." I did. "Lean forward, and rest your hands on the window sill."

The window was almost three feet away. I had to bend sharply at the waist for my hands to reach comfortably. The curtains were closed so we had privacy. It kept the room dim, too, which let me be more open and less self-conscious.

"Spread your legs apart." I hesitated, still slightly unsure. I was completely naked, bent over. I was exposed and vulnerable. He caressed my lower back, which sent a jolt of pleasure through me. My core started to throb, demanding to be touched. Still leaning forward, I opened my legs.

"Wider." I opened them wide enough to feel cool air on my hot center.

"Oh, my god." He put his hands on my lower back and ran them gently across my hips, my ass, and down the sides of my legs. He held the cheeks of my ass in his hands and massaged me until I was bending even lower, opening myself up to him. I needed him deep inside me.

He moved his hands lower, and ran them back up my inner thighs. He stopped just beneath my swollen wet center. I waited and whimpered. He moved further up, and when he reached my cleft, his fingers parted me, then ran along the edges and ridges of my flesh, until they just grazed my clitoris. His thumbs entered me and began a gentle rocking, in and out.

My head dropped and I pushed back onto his hands, wanting him deeper and deeper. Suddenly, though, the movements stopped. He took his hands away, and I was left hot and dissatisfied. He was moving back, away from me. I stood up, covering myself with my hands, "What's wrong?"

He was shaking his head and trying to cover his erection. "Nothing, Maddie. Nothing at all. You look so sexy..."

"But?"

"But, this isn't right." He wrapped me in the blanket from the sofa. "This is not how this morning should end. I want to take you out. I want to go to a great restaurant, an elegant restaurant, I want to talk to you, maybe kiss you once or twice." He moved to me and kissed me on the lips, twice. "And after we've had a nice meal, I want to come back and make love to you like we did last night. And after all that, then, we can do what we were just about to do."

"For dessert?"

He laughed, "Yes. This can be dessert. But this isn't all we are to each other, right? I want to start with a date, a first date. If I have my way it will be the last first date you ever go on."

I looked into his eyes and saw that he meant it. We were going to make this work. He was mine and I was his. We needed to take our time, to treasure what we had found. What we had fought for.

"That sounds really wonderful. But I don't have an elegant outfit for an elegant date." I swirled around, modeling the blanket for him Scarlett O'Hara style.

"I'm sure you have something."

"No, I really don't." I stopped swirling. "After the thing with Brandon and the pictures, I threw away everything remotely pretty. Except one dress, which I wore to Owen's. And you know what happened to that one."

He nodded and I knew he remembered me silently dumping it into the trash.

"Well," he was rubbing his hands together. "Let's go shopping."

I looked at him skeptically. "Shopping? What happened to the tough guy?"

"My baby needs a dress!"

"Baby has no money. Look, I'm really not trying to be a downer, I promise. But I don't have any extra money. Cab fare from Owen's was my food budget for the week. Things are tight. Can't we go somewhere for a nice meal where I can just wear what I have?"

He shook his head. "No. No way. That is not my vision." I couldn't help laughing. He was all man, but this little daydream had him caught in its grasp. He was going to be a real groomzilla someday. "I have money. Enough, anyway. Let's get something!"

I sat down with a sigh. I was getting frustrated. "How is our romantic day turning into a scene from Pretty Woman? You're being very sweet, but I don't want to go from store to store trying on things that look terrible until we're both tired and cranky. That is the opposite of sexy and romantic."

He left the room. I was worried we were having an argument, but he came back with the half-read novel I had left on my bedside table. He tucked the blanket in around me, even under my toes, and handed me the book.

"I will be back in an hour. With clothing. Which you will wear." End of discussion, I guess.

"Wait a minute. We're all, you know, hot and bothered. Aren't you going to do something?"

"No, I'm not and neither are you. Let's stay 'hot and bothered' all day, and by the time we get back home, we'll be tearing each other's clothes off." He smiled widely at the visual.

I smiled, too: partly at the thought of the next three hours of foreplay, but mainly at having heard him say that we would be coming home. We. Home. I had somehow managed to build my-

self a tiny family after all. I gave him a quick kiss and waved
him off.

CHAPTER FORTY-SEVEN

He got his coat on and left. I wanted to start reading right away, but had a couple of phone calls to make first. I wanted to have everything taken care of so that when Liam got back, nothing would be in the way.

I called PICU and talked to a nurse about Alex. He was stabilizing well. Even his kidney function had improved. I told her I'd be in the next day to see him, and if his parents needed to talk, she could page me any time.

Next, I called Isabel. She wasn't in, but her Mom wanted to talk. They weren't sure what they were going to do. She told me that Owen had taken sick leave from the hospital, but that they hadn't pressed any charges yet. I was sure they had been told all about how unlikely a court case was to win, and how devastating it could all be for Isabel. It would be devastating either way, though, and I hoped they got to do whatever felt right and was best for them.

I mentioned that I wanted to pass the photographs I had on to someone else. I didn't want them on my phone, or in my possession at all. She asked me to send them on to their lawyer. I told her I'd check in with Isabel to make sure she was on board with the plan and then I'd email them right away. I reassured her, again, that I would be deleting them from my files immediately afterwards.

I wasn't sure what I was going to do about Owen. It really came down to what Isabel decided to do. I had to put it out of my mind. Nothing was going to ruin this day with Liam.

I got up from the sofa to have some water, brush my teeth, and put on a little makeup.

Liam had been gone just over an hour. There were several stores close by, but I had never been in most of them. I had no idea what kind of clothes they had. I was pretty sure he would have the wrong sizes, and the dress would probably be something a stripper would wear. Well, it would be fun to play dress up. And then put on my normal clothes and go out for a very late lunch.

I had just settled back into the blanket, ready to finally start in on my book, when Liam returned with several bags. He walked to my bedroom and put the bags on my bed. I followed behind. "All yours, Mademoiselle."

"All right. Let's do this." I closed the door, with Liam on the other side, and started poking through the bags. I was really hoping there would be at least one piece of clothing I could put on. I wanted to be a good sport.

I recognized the lingerie store's name on one of the bags. I peeked inside. There was a bra and panty set. Deep-red lace. I had tried it on before and loved it. I opened the door and called out to Liam, "You've got a lot of confidence, buying a woman lingerie."

"What, it's just underwear," he called back. "I know what you look like. I bought you a bathing suit, remember? It's no big deal."

I looked down at the set. Even the sizes were perfect. Liam continued, "And the sales lady remembered you, so that helped."

I had a number of questions about that, but they could wait. At least I was able to wear the 'underwear' he had chosen. I put it on, and noticed there was also a garter at the bottom. I will admit that I think these are wildly sexy and had always wanted to have one. To have beautiful stockings reaching just to the top of my thighs, and clipped precariously in place. I shivered imagining Liam's fingers undoing them later. Another bag revealed the stockings. They were whisper thin and silky soft.

INVITATION

The dress took my breath away. It was a delicate black lace sheath, misleadingly simple to look at, but so beautiful on. It had a V-neck, cut much lower than I had worn before, but it was tasteful and sensuous. I felt like a really sexy Audrey Hepburn.

He had even thought of shoes, which was very lucky, since mine were mostly practical pairs meant to be worn for hours while I raced around the hospital. The ones Liam had chosen were insanely expensive and, of course, the right size. They were pretty black patent leather with slender three inch heels; maybe a touch too high for an afternoon lunch date, but subtly sexy. With the dress they were perfection. When I put them on, I suddenly had supermodel legs.

I put my blonde hair up in a loose French twist. I changed my pinkish lipstick for a soft red that went well with the black of the dress. For jewelry, I had on my tiny diamond stud earrings, but nothing else. I didn't own anything else. My Dad had my Mom's jewelry: a sad story for another time.

I stood staring at myself in the mirror. I looked like myself, my old self, the one who had liked life and who had sought out adventures. My old self had never been particularly confident, but I had at least been able to feel pretty when I dressed up. It had been so long since I had put effort into my appearance. I looked like my old self, but better, because I had a glow, the glow of someone who loves and is loved back.

Liam poked his head in the door. Our eyes met it the full-length mirror. He held my gaze for several seconds, seeing the happiness and love there. I turned to face him.

"You look so beautiful." He spoke with longing and love and happiness.

"Thank you for this. For all of this." I walked to him and he pulled me into a tight embrace.

I leaned back. "How did you get everything so right?"

He shrugged. "The underwear lady helped me. She told me what size you would probably wear. I told her about our date, so she went on the computer to look for the perfect dress for lunch at my new favorite restaurant. We found the dress at a store down the street, and I ran and got it. She was like one of those grandmas in a Disney movie."

I had to think about that one for a second. "Oh, Fairy God-mothers! Yes, she is exactly like a Fairy Godmother. I have dibs on her. I met her first."

"Okay," he smiled. "That seems fair."

"And the shoes?"

"Checked your size on the way out the door."

"Ah. Old-school detective work. Nice. Well, everything is just perfect. Thank you so much."

He stepped back from me a bit and looked at my neck and chest. "Not quite perfect. The saleswoman said this neckline needs a necklace." He ran his fingers across the expanse of bare skin. I shivered with pleasure.

"Sorry. Don't have that either." I felt a little embarrassed, but I *had* told him that I didn't have expensive things.

"Yes, you do." His face grew serious. He pulled a rectangular box from his pocket. "It's not fancy, but I want you to remember our night."

I looked into his eyes. "I'm not going to forget tonight."

He opened the box and held it out to me. I pulled back from it a little. "You're not going to snap my fingers with it, are you? Because that would be going too far, and would definitely ruin the moment."

He looked confused. "What do you mean? What are you talking about?"

"In the movie..."

"What movie?"

I realized that, of course, the likelihood of his having seen Pretty Woman was pretty much zero. It made his having come up with all this even sweeter.

"Nothing, never mind. My mistake." I picked up the delicate chain.

It was white gold, with a small diamond pendant. Simple and lovely. I thought it was perfect, but it was much too early in our relationship to be accepting gifts like that.

"It is absolutely beautiful, but it's too extravagant. I can't take this. I shouldn't even be taking these shoes." I tried to put the necklace back in the box. I wanted to do the right thing, but I felt the magic of the moment slipping away.

"Let me do this. Please. It means so much to me." Liam took the necklace from my hands and moved behind me. He gently pushed the small hairs at the nape of my neck out of the way, and did up the clasp.

He came back around, took my face in his hands and kissed me. He put his forehead against mine. "I love you." I could only nod and stroke his hair. I was too overcome with emotion to talk.

We pulled away from each other reluctantly. He got my coat from the closet and helped me put it on. He put his own coat on, and then looped his elbow around mine. "Shall we?" he asked.

I wanted to ask one more question. "Why did you tell the sales woman that it was your new favorite restaurant?"

"Because it's where we're going on our first date." He looked at me as though he was having to state the most obvious of things.

"My last first date?"

He grew serious then. He moved in front of me so I was facing him. He put one arm beside my face and one in the small of my back. He pulled me to him and kissed me gently, then harder, passionately and hungrily, like a soldier who has finally come home. "Does that answer your question?"

I smiled and looked up at him. I tried to pour all the love and happiness I was feeling into my gaze, so he could see and feel it, too.

There was a little of my red lipstick on him, and I wiped it off tenderly.

I held his hand and opened the door. We would have a beautiful dinner. We would talk and laugh and kiss. We would spend the night exploring our bodies and our new love. My last first date was about to begin, and I could hardly wait.

Hello Readers,

So, how was it for *you*?!
As an indie (Independent) author I rely on your reviews to help spread the word about my book. Reviews also help me to become a better writer.

If you have a moment, and are willing to write an honest review, please click here:

Amazon Author Page:
http://www.amazon.com/author/christinahoffman

Or here on Goodreads:
https://www.goodreads.com/goodreadscomsmart_sexy

Reviews submitted in April, May and June 2014 will all be entered into a drawing for an Amazon Gift Card (Three in total. One for each month).

I value all reviews, and a "good" review is not required for entry. Simply submit a review, then visit my website or send me an email letting me know you've done so. The information is below.

I will also be having regular giveaways at Goodreads (author page) and on my website ChristinaHoffman.com. So, join us for updates, prizes and fun.

Thank you all,

Christina

Christinahoffman.com

http://twitter.com/choffmanbooks

ChristinaHoffmanbooks@gmail.com

https://www.facebook.com/christina.hoffman.smartandsexy

ABOUT THE AUTHOR

Christina Hoffman was born in London, England. She moved with her family throughout Canada and the US, and has finally put down her suitcase, for now, in San Francisco.

She believes that everyone has the right to feel both smart and sexy. We don't have to be one or the other! She writes stories about characters who live in the real world and who, somehow, incredibly, still believe in love.

She's starting a mini-revolution. She writes sexy stories, but hasn't forgotten the romance in her Romances. Enough with whips -- back to lips!

She hopes you enjoy her stories and see yourself in her characters. After all, they are based on smart and sexy people, just like you.